Dear Reader,

Welcome to book two of my duet OUTBACK MARRIAGES. I hope when you've read both stories you'll be able to say with satisfaction, "I really enjoyed them!" Better yet "And I actually learned something I didn't know before!"

A devoted fan recently asked me what inspired me to write so much about the Outback when I wasn't born there. True, I was born in subtropical Brisbane, a city I love, but when I was a girl I went to a prestigious school called All Hallows. All Hallows took in boarders from all over Queensland's vast Outback. These girls had something special about them. When I used to listen to their stories of "home," I was fascinated. They came from places with legendary names like Longreach, Thargominda and Cloncurry, birthplace of QANTAS—Queensland and Northern Territory Aerial Services—and the Royal Flying Doctor Service, which spread its mantle of safety all over the Outback.

I was introduced to billowing red dust storms, drought, flood, the Dreamtime, Aborigines, billabongs, brumbies, camels, dingoes, private planes and governesses when they were small. For the highly imaginative girl I was, the Outback assumed near-mythical proportions in my mind. As a woman I discovered for myself reality not only matched those stories, it exceeded them. I had to see those amazing dry but vivid, burned ocher colors for myself. Our Australian Outback truly does have an incredible mystique. For the majority of you who can't possibly visit, I hope I've succeeded in opening a window on this unique part of the world.

Best wishes to you all, and a very special thank-you to my longtime loyal fans who have given me so much support throughout my long career. If we didn't have readers, we wouldn't have writers! Take a bow!

Margaret Way

She was walking toward him, graciously extending a long, delicate hand.

"How do you do?" she said in a husky voice.

She didn't smile at him, coolly summing him up. He didn't smile at her. Instead they studied one another with an absolute thoroughness that seemed to lock out everyone else in the room.

She looked away first.

He didn't know how to interpret that. A win or a loss?

MARGARET WAY
Cattle Rancher, Convenient Wife

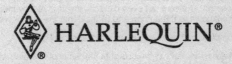

HARLEQUIN®

TORONTO • NEW YORK • LONDON
AMSTERDAM • PARIS • SYDNEY • HAMBURG
STOCKHOLM • ATHENS • TOKYO • MILAN • MADRID
PRAGUE • WARSAW • BUDAPEST • AUCKLAND

ISBN-13: 978-0-373-03937-1
ISBN-10: 0-373-03937-9

CATTLE RANCHER, CONVENIENT WIFE

First North American Publication 2007.

Copyright © 2007 by Margaret Way, Pty., Ltd.

www.eHarlequin.com

Printed in U.S.A.

OUTBACK MARRIAGES
These bush bachelors are looking for a bride!

Welcome to Jimboorie—a friendly Outback town that sits amongst the striking red rocky landscape in the heart of Australia. This is where two rugged ranchers begin their quest for marriage.

Meet Clay Cunningham and Rory Compton—they're each searching for a wife. But will they find the right woman with whom to spend the rest of their lives?

Find out in this new duet from Margaret Way!

Last time, you met Clay in
Outback Man Seeks Wife

And now you can read Rory's story!
Cattle Rancher, Convenient Wife

Margaret Way takes great pleasure in her work, and works hard at her pleasure. She enjoys tearing off to the beach with her family on weekends, loves haunting galleries and auctions and is completely given over to French champagne "for every possible joyous occasion." She was born and educated in the river city of Brisbane, Australia, and now lives within sight and sound of beautiful Moreton Bay.

Books by Margaret Way

HARLEQUIN ROMANCE
OUTBACK MAN SEEKS WIFE*
HER OUTBACK PROTECTOR
THE CATTLE BARON'S BRIDE

*Outback Marriages

CHAPTER ONE

THOUGH his mood was fairly grim Rory Compton couldn't help but smile. It was the middle of the day, yet a man could fire a cannon down the main street of Jimboorie and not find a target; not even a stray dog. The broad sunlit street was deserted as were the sidewalks, usually ganged on a Saturday. No kids were bobbing, weaving, ducking about, playing some private game, while their mothers, looking harried shouted at them to stop. No one was loading groceries into the family pickup. No dusty four-wheel drive's ran back and forth, the drivers waving casually and calling greetings to friends and acquaintances which meant pretty well everyone in town.

Seated on the upper verandah of Vince Dougherty's pub, Rory had the perfect view of the town centre, its impressive community Hall and its attractive park. He drained off the cold beer he'd enjoyed with the prepacked lunch Dougherty's wife, Katie, had very kindly left him; a plate of thick roast beef and pickles sandwiches, cling wrapped so well it took him almost five minutes to get into it. He hadn't a hope of working his way through the pile. The stray dog would have come in handy in that regard. With the possible exception of himself, the whole town had taken itself off to the big 'open day' on Jimboorie, an outlying historic sheep station that had given the town its name. Sitting there, his long legs resting on planter's chair, he debated whether to go. There was a sli chance it could boost his mood.

It was a restoration party he understood from Vince, wh being a publican was always ready for a chat that naturall included dramatic revelations. The old homestead, from a accounts, once magnificent, had been allowed to go to rac and ruin under the custodianship of the former owner, Angu Cunningham. 'A miserable old bastard! Didn't think anyor in town was good enough to talk to!'

Of course Rory knew the name Cunningham. Th Cunninghams figured among the roll call Outback pioneer Sheep men. Not cattlemen like his own kind, their stampin ground, the legendary Channel Country, a riverine desert dee into the South-West pocket of their vast State. The new owne a great nephew, 'one helluva guy!' had spent well over a ye and a mountain of money restoring the place. Lucky old hin Vince had invited Rory along to the open day—'Sure and the won't mind!' Vince was as expansive as though he an Cunningham were best mates.

'Maybe,' he'd said. And maybe not. He wasn't in his be spirits since he and his father had had their cataclysmic ro a couple of weeks back. Since then he'd been on the road travelling from one Outback town to another in a sick, angr daze, checking out if there were any pastoral properties on th market he could afford with the help of a hefty bank loan. H couldn't lift his eyes to the multimillion range. All up inclu ing the private nest egg his grandad, Trevis Compton, had le him he had close to two million dollars A lot of money to lot of people. Not near enough when one was talking halfway decent pastoral property.

'I haven't left your brother, Jay, anything outside th personal things he loves,' Trevis had told him years bac

They were sitting on the front steps watching another glorious desert sunset, his grandad's arm around his shoulder. 'Jay's the heir. He gets Turrawin. It's always been that way. The eldest Compton son inherits to ensure the family heritage is kept intact. There are problems with splitting it a number of ways. Jay's a good boy. I love him dearly. But he's not *you*. You're meant for big things, Rory. A little nest egg might well come in handy after I'm gone.'

Rory could still hear his grandfather's deep gentle voice. How could two men be so different? His grandfather and his dad? To be strictly fair his grandfather had led a charmed life with a devoted wife as his constant companion. His son Bernard, however, had his life blighted fairly early. Bitterness ate into a man's soul. That last row had been one row too many. On both sides. His father had sent him on his way— hell he was going anyway—hurling the most vicious and unjust insults that even Rory, used to his father's ungovernable tirades, was deeply shocked. He had passed his elder brother, Jay, his father's heir in the entrance hall.

'Damn him, damn him! Damn him to hell!' Jay was muttering, white faced and shamed, furious with his father for attacking Rory but unprepared to go to his defence. Their father had turned big strong Jay into a powder puff, Rory thought sadly. Anyway Jay's intervention would have been in vain. He was going or his own pride and integrity would be hopelessly compromised. What did it matter he ran Turrawin these days and largely for the past four years? His father wanted him *out*! Sometimes Rory thought his father couldn't abide to look at him.

They had never been close. Instinctively Rory had known the reason. He strongly resembled his mother who had run off and left her husband and children when Rory was twelve and Jay fourteen. A *really* bad time. It had brought scandal on the family and a very hard life on Laura Compton's two boys who had worshipped her. From that day forward their father had succumbed to the dark places that were in him. His temper, always volatile became so uncontrollable his young sons lived in a constant state of fear and anxiety. Jay was often in floods of tears after a beating with a riding crop; Rory, *never* which only served to inflame their father further. Both boys regarded boarding school as a god-send. By the age of sixteen and eighteen, both six foot plus, taller and stronger than their father, the beatings had stopped. Their father had been forced to turn his attention back to his whiplash tongue.

'As soon as Dad's dead you and I are going to be full partners,' Jay had promised, his voice full of brotherly love and *pride*. Jay made no bones about it. Rory was everything he was not. 'I won't be able to run Turrawin without you. We both know that. The men look to you not me. *You're* the cattleman. The man to save the station. Dad didn't inherit Grandad's skills or his leadership qualities. Neither did I You're the *real* cattleman, Rory.'

Rory sighed deeply knowing Jay would get into trouble without him. Bernard Compton had bruised his sons badly But he hasn't beaten *me*, Rory thought determinedly. I've go everything going for me. Youth, health, strength, the necessary skills. He'd start up his own run. Move up in easy stages He was as ready to found a dynasty as his Compton ancestors had before him. In time—it would have to be pretty soon he'd turned twenty-eight—he'd find himself a wife. A young woman reared to the Outback. A woman with a deep love c the land who could withstand an isolated existence withou caving in to depression or a mad craving for city lights.

Romantic love wasn't all that high on his agenda. Romance had a shelf life. That was the down side. He had to learn fron experience. Most people didn't. History wasn't going 1 repeat itself with him. His best bet was a *partner* who coul go the distance. That meant for *life*; a contractual sort of arrangement that the two of them would honour, working strongly together to build a future. As long as the woman was young and reasonably attractive the sex should be okay. He definitely wanted children. He knew he wasn't and never could be a hard, cruel bastard like his old man. He would be a good father to his children, not bring them up in a minefield. The Outback certainly bred hard men, *tough* men. But mercifully not many like his dad.

So what to do now? Rory stood up and stretched his long arms, staring down at the empty street. He had plenty of time on his hands. Why not take a run out to Jimboorie?

He might as well. Vince had given him directions. A beautiful old homestead would be worth seeing at least. It might even offer some comfort. He'd been intrigued to learn the new owner's Christian name was Clay. Clay Cunningham. He'd only ever met one Clay in his life, but that was a Clay Dyson, the overseer on Havilah a couple of years back. A guy around his own age held in great esteem by his employer, old Colonel Forbes, ex-British Army, now deceased, who had inherited Havilah from his Australian cousin and to everyone's astonishment had remained in the country to work it. Colonel Forbes, universally respected, had thought the world of Clay Dyson, Rory recalled. But it wasn't *that* Clay. Couldn't be. The Clay Dyson he had known had no background of money, no family *name*, though the word was old Colonel Forbes had remembered him in his will.

By the time he arrived on Jimboorie, a splendid property and as far out of his reach as planet Pluto, the main compound was still crowded with people but some were starting to leave making for the parking area crammed with vehicles of all makes and price tags. During the long approach to the station he had seen more than one light aircraft airborne, heading home. He made a quick tour of the very extensive gardens marvelling at the great design and the rich variety of trees, flowering plants and shrubs he presumed were drought tolerant and could withstand dust storms.

Beneath a long tunnel of cerise bouganvillea that blossomed heavily over an all but smothered green wrought-iron trellis, he passed two pretty young women from the town who smiled at him shyly in acknowledgement. He smiled back, raising a hand in salute, totally unaware it only took an instant for his smile to light up his entire face and dispel the dark, serious, brooding look he'd worn since his teens.

Jimboorie House impressed him immensely. He'd never expected it to be so *big* or so grand. It was huge! It rivalled if not surpassed any of the historic homesteads he had been invited into over the years. When his mother had been with them—when they were *family*—they had been invited everywhere as a matter or course. His beautiful mother, Laura, had been very popular, herself an excellent hostess presiding over their own handsome homestead on which she had lavished much love and care.

Why then had she abandoned them? Didn't God decree mothers had to remain with their children? For years he and Jay had accepted the reason their father had drummed into them. City bred their mother had only awaited the opportunity when they were old enough to renounce her lonely Outback life. As young men they came to understand what life for their mother might have been like, though their father had been reasonably enough *then*. Well, for most of the time anyway. He had never actually laid a hand on them when their mother was around except for the odd time when she had protested so strongly he had stopped. In any event she had remarried after the divorce. That happened all the time but it was lousy for the kids.

Their father, as was to be expected given his name, his
oney and influence, gained custody. He had never been
epared to share it with his ex-wife. The failure of their
arriage was her fault entirely. It was one of his father's most
arked characteristics, he held himself blameless in all things.
heir mother alone deserved condemnation. The sharing was
bad idea anyway. Sensitive Jay had always become enor-
ously upset when it was time to leave her. Equally upset,
ough he never let on, Rory behaved badly. He had to take
e pain out on someone. He had chosen to take it out on his
other. After a while the visits became farther and farther in-
tween, then ceased altogether.

'Didn't I tell you?' their father had crowed, that hard tri-
mphant gleam in his eyes as he started all over again to trash
eir mother. 'She doesn't want you. She never did! She's a
lfish, self-centred heartless bitch! We're well rid of her!'

Neither of them would have won a good parenting award,
ory thought. But well rid of her? People really did die
om grief. All three of them, father and sons, hadn't been
le to handle her desertion. Their father, a proud and
rogant man, had never been free of his own grief and
azed thoughts of personal humiliation. Rory's memories
his mother were so heartwrenching he rarely allowed
em to touch him. He and Jay had believed their mother to
e the sweetest, gentlest, funniest, mother in the world. She
uld always make them laugh. It just didn't seem possible
e had been faking it as their father always claimed.
evertheless she had left, taking no account of the devasta-
n she left behind her.

In choosing a woman of his own, Rory had long since
cided he had to make absolutely sure he kept his eyes and
rs open and his feet firmly on the ground. He was as sus-
ptible to a woman's beauty as the next man—maybe more

so he thought wryly—but there was no way he was going
allow himself to be seduced by it.

Or so he thought.

Vince Dougherty caught sight of him as he was wandering
grandly proportioned rooms of the old homestead letting
work its magic on him. Whoever had been responsible for
interior decoration—probably a top city designer—had d
a great job.

'You made it!' Vince, looking delighted—his enthusia
was hard to resist—made a beeline for him pumping his ha
as though he hadn't seen him for weeks instead of arou
eight-thirty that morning. 'What d'yah think now? Tell n
He poked Rory's shoulder which was marginally better th
a poke in the ribs. 'You look like a guy with good taste.'

'That's very kind of you, Vince.' Rory's answer w
laconic. 'It's magnificent!' His admiration was unfeign
'Definitely well worth the visit!'

Vince looked as proud as if he were the owner, decora
landscaper, all rolled into one. The kind of guy who chang
lives. 'Told yah, didn't I? You should have come an hour
so earlier. Meet the Cunninghams yet?'

'Not so far.' Rory shook his head. 'I only came to
the house really. I'm only passing through, Vince. Just I
I told you.'

'Well, yah never know!' Vince's face creased into anot
smile. He was hoping this fine-looking young fella would s
in the district. He glanced upwards to the gallery. 'Tha
Carrie, Mrs Cunningham up there.' Discreetly he pointed
a blond young woman with a lovely innocent face an
radiant smile. She was standing in the midst of a circle
women friends who were laughing at something she w
saying, which they obviously found very funny.

Rory could understand Vince's look of undying admiration. 'She's very beautiful,' he said. 'The house suits her perfectly.'

Vince's big amiable face settled into an expression of pride. 'An angel!' he announced. 'Clay reckons he's the luckiest man in the world. Now how about me taking you to find him? I reckon you young blokes would get on.'

Why not? 'Just point me in his direction, Vince,' Rory said. 'I see your wife beckoning to you.'

'My little sweetheart!' Vince exclaimed, a tag Rory had heard at least forty times during his stay. Vince and Katie were apparently right for each other. Katie wasn't *little*, either. 'Have to get back to the pub sooner or later. Try outdoors, near the fountain. Clay was there a few minutes ago. I don't think he's come back into the house.'

'Will do.' Rory tipped a finger to his temple.

It would turn out to be one of the best moves he had ever made.

The marble three-tiered fountain, monumental in size to suit the grand proportions of the house, was playing; an object of fascination for the children who had to be dragged away from the water by their mothers before they fell in or climbed in as one daring six-year-old had already done and been lightly chastised for. At such times he always remembered how his father had used to bawl him out as a child. It seemed like he had always made his father mad. Madder and madder as the years wore on. And later after their grandad died, the blind rages that took longer and longer to blow over.

A tall, handsome young man stood like a monarch at the top of the broad sloping lawn that ran down to a sun spangled creek. White lilies were blooming all around the banks, an exquisite foil for the sparkling stream and the green foliage of

the reeds and the myriad water plants. Rory walked towar
him, his spirits growing lighter. Surely it was Clay Dyson
Dyson was an arresting looking guy, hard to miss. Rory l
his amazement show on his face.

'It *is* Clay, isn't it? Clay Dyson?' he called. 'Used to b
overseer on Havilah a couple of years back?'

The other man turned, his face breaking into a smile c
surprise as he recognised his visitor. He walked toward Ror
thrusting out a welcoming hand. 'Cunningham now, Ror
Cunningham is my *real* name by the way. How are you an
what are you doing so far from home?' he exclaimed. 'Nc
that it isn't great to see you.'

'Great to see you!' Rory responded in kind, returning th
handshake. He hadn't known Clay Dyson—Cunningha
whatever—all that well, but what he'd seen and what he'
heard he'd liked. 'So what's the story, Clay? And this home
stead!' He turned to gaze towards the front facade. 'It'
magnificent.'

'It is,' Clay agreed with serene pride. 'There is a story, c
course. A long one. I'll tell you sometime, but to cut it sho
it all came about through a bitter family feud. You knov
about them?'

'I do.' Rory made a wry face.

'Mercifully the feud has been put to bed,' Clay said wit
satisfaction. 'My great-uncle Angus left me all this.' He threv
out his arm with a flourish. 'Caroline, my wife, and I hav
only recently called a halt to renovations. They were might
extensive and mighty expensive. What I inherited was a fa
cry from what you see now.'

'So I believe,' Rory said in an admiring voice. 'I'm stayin
at the Jimboorie pub for a few days. Vince told me about th
open day out here. I'm glad I came.'

'So am I.' Clay smiled. 'Have you met Caroline yet?'

'The very beautiful blonde with the big brown eyes?' Rory gave the other man a sideways grin.

'That's Caroline!' Clay couldn't keep the proud smile off his face.

'I haven't had the pleasure,' Rory said. 'You're one lucky guy, Cunningham.'

'You should talk!' Clay scoffed, totally unaware of Rory's changed circumstances. 'How's Jay isn't it, and your dad?'

'Jay's fine. He's the heir. My dad and I had one helluva bust up. That's why I'm on the road.'

Clay was aware of the pain and anger behind the easy conversational tone. 'That's rough! I'm sorry to hear it.' The Comptons had been an eminent Channel Country cattle family for generations. Where did that leave Rory?

'It was a long time coming,' Rory told him calmly. 'I didn't have any choice but to hit the road. I have some money set aside from my grandad. I guess he knew in his bones I might be in need of it sometime. What I'm looking for now is a spread of my own. Nothing like Jimboorie of course. I'm nowhere in your league, but a nice little run I can bring up to scratch and sell off as I move up the chain.'

Clay looked down to the creek, where children were running and shrieking, overexcited. 'No chance your dad will cool off, Rory? Could there be a reconciliation?'

Rory uncovered his head, his thick wavy hair as black and glossy as a magpie's wing. A lock fell forward on his darkly tanned forehead. 'No way! I wouldn't care if he did. That part of my life is over. The only thing I'm sorry about is I'm leaving Jay to it.'

Clay studied Rory with a thoughtful frown. He remembered now the Compton family history. 'You know I might be able to help you,' Clay confided, like someone who already had an idea in his mind, which indeed he did. 'Why don't you come back inside? Meet Caroline. Stay to dinner. A few friends are stopping over. I'd like you to meet them. You're not desperate to get back to town are you?'

'Heck no!' Rory felt a whole lot better in two minutes flat. 'I'd love to stay if it's okay with your beautiful wife?'

'It'll be fine!' Clay assured him, following his gut feeling about Rory Compton. This was a guy he could trust; a guy who could make a good friend. 'Caroline will be happy to meet you. And we'll have time to catch up.'

'Great!' A surge of pleasure at Clay's hospitality ran through him. Rory whipped out his transforming smile.

Destiny has an amazing way of throwing people together.

CHAPTER TWO

RORY found it all too easy to settle into the spacious, high-ceilinged guest bedroom that had been allotted him. His room at the pub, albeit clean and comfortable was *tiny* for a guy his size.

'Stay the night, Rory,' Clay had insisted. 'We'll be having a few drinks over dinner. Anyway it's too far to drive back into own. Everyone else is staying over until morning. There's any mount of room. Twelve bedrooms in, although we haven't got around to furnishing the lot as yet.'

His bedroom had a beautiful dark hardwood floor, partially overed by a stylish modern rug in cream and brown. Teak urnishings with clean Asian lines gave the room its 'masculine' feel. The colour scheme was elegant and subdued, the edspread, the drapery fabric and the cushions on the long ofa of a golden beige Thai silk. It was all very classy. Clay ad even lent him a shirt to wear to dinner. Something 'dressier' since he'd only been wearing a short-sleeved bush hirt. They were much of a height and build. In fact the shirt tted perfectly.

Drinks were being served in the refurbished drawing room seven. It was almost that now. He'd showered and washed s hair using the shampoo in the well-stocked cabinet. Now he ave himself a quick glance in the mirror aware as always of

his resemblance to his mother. He had her thick sable hair, h
olive skin, though life in the open air had tanned his to bronz
It was *her* eyes looking back at him; the setting, the colour. The
flashed silver against his darkened skin. He had her clean bor
structure, the high cheekbones, the jawline, stronger and mo
definite in him. Hell his face was *angular* now he came to tal
a good look. He'd lost a bit of weight stressing over the curre
situation and being forever on the road. Who would have eve
thought it bad luck to closely resemble his beautiful mother
Although their old man had scarcely liked Jay more, when Ja
was almost a double for their father at the same age. Jay cou
never be brutal. Jay was a lovely human being who really wasn
born to raise cattle. Both straight A students at their 'old money
boarding school Jay had once spoken of a desire to stud
medicine. It had only brought forth ridicule and high scor
from their father while their mother had gone to Jay laying h
smooth cheek against his.

'And you'd be a fine doctor, Jay. Your grandfather Eugen
was a highly respected orthopaedic surgeon.'

'Stop it, Laura!' their father had thundered, his handson
face as hard as granite. 'Mollycoddling the boy as usua
Putting ideas into his head. There's no place for nonsens
here. Jay is my *heir*! His life is here on Turrawin. Let that l
an end to it.'

His expression darkened with remembrance. He missed h
brother. Their father would blame Jay for every last littl
thing that went wrong now. It was dreadful to wish your ow
father would just ride off into the sunset and never come bac
but both of his sons were guilty of wanting that in their mind

'You *are* a sick bastard, aren't you?' he berated himsel
making a huge effort to throw off his mood. He'd already m
most of his dinner companions, which was good. No surpris
there. They were all nice, friendly people around his ag

aybe a year or two older. Two married couples, the Stapletons
d the Mastermans and a young woman, called Chloe Sanders
th softly curling brown hair and big sky-blue eyes whose face
came highly flushed when he spoke to her. Perhaps she was
ercome with shyness, though she had to be well into her
enties and maybe past the time for hectic blushes.

It appeared there was a sister, Allegra, who was staying
er as well, but so far she hadn't appeared. Caroline had told
m in a quiet aside Allegra, recently divorced, was under-
ndably feeling a bit low. She was staying a while with her
ther and sister on the family property, Naroom, which *just
uld* be up for sale. A hint there surely? The girls' father, Llew
nders had contracted a very bad strain of malaria while on
isit to New Guinea. Complications had set in but by the time
was properly hospitalised it was already too late. That was
months back, around the time Allegra's divorce had been
ialised. All three women had been shattered, Caroline told
m, her lovely face compassionate. The daughter who had
yed at home with her parents was Chloe. The one with the
cy name, Allegra, had flown the coup to marry a high
ing Sydney stockbroker then had turned around and
orced him within a few years. Rory didn't get it. She was
young for a midlife crisis. Why did she marry at all if she
dn't been prepared to make a go of it? Then again to be fair
might have been the husband's fault? If the sisters looked
ything alike, and they probably did, the high flyer husband
uld well have found someone more glamorous and exciting?
*Heaven help me, I might like a bit of glamour and excite-
nt myself!*

Rory didn't want to know it, but he was a man at war
th himself.

They were all assembled in the drawing room, chatting
sily together, drinks in hand.

'Ah, there you are, Rory. What's it to be?' Clay as
'I've made a pitcher of ice-cold martinis if you're intereste

'They're very good!' Meryl Stapleton held up her glass. '(
told me his secret. Just show the vermouth bottle to the gin

Rory laughed. 'I'm not a great one for cocktails, I'm afr

'A beer then?' Clay produced a top brand.

'Fine.' Rory smiled and went to sit beside Chloe who
sending out silent but unmistakable signals. A man co
learn a lot from a woman who wanted him to sit beside
She flushed up prettily and shifted her rounded botton
make a place for him. Still no sign of the sister. Perhaps
was all damped down with depression? Maybe their hos
would have to go to her and offer a little encouragement

Greg Stapleton, a slightly avid expression on his face,
mediately started into asking him if he was any relation to
Channel Country Comptons. 'You know the cattle dynas

Obviously Clay hadn't filled him in. Rory was grateful
that. He really didn't want to talk about his family. Neverthe
he found himself nodding casually. 'The very same, Greg.

'Say that's great!' Greg Stapleton gazed back at him v
heightened interest. 'But what are you doing in this nec
the woods? You'd be way out of your territory?'

Rory answered pleasantly though he wanted to
'That's *it*!'

'Actually, Greg, I'm looking to start up on my own.'

Stapleton look amazed. 'Glory be! When Turrawin is
of our major cattle stations? The biggest and the best in
nation. Surely you'd have more than enough to do there'

'I have an elder brother, Greg,' Rory said, making it so
like it was no big deal instead of a boot out the door situat
'Jay's my father's heir. Not me. I've always wanted to do
own thing.'

'And I'm sure you'll be marvellous at it,' Chloe spoke

otectively and gently touched his arm. Chloe it appeared was ery sympathetic young woman. Nothing wrong with that!

'I'm totally against this primogeniture thing!' Greg announced. 'It's all wrong and it's hopelessly archaic.'

'Ah, here's Allegra!' Caroline rose gracefully to her feet, ateful for the intervention her guest's arrival presented. Clay d told her in advance a little of Rory Compton's story so e knew he wouldn't want to talk about it. But there was no pping Greg once he got started. She welcomed the wcomer to their midst. 'Just in time for a drink before mer, Allegra!'

'That would be lovely!' A faintly husky, marvellously sexy, ice responded.

My God, what a turn up!

Rory just managed to hold himself back from outright ring. He was absolutely certain *this* femme fatale had left t just a husband but a string of broken hearts in her wake. had enough presence of mind to rise to his feet along with other men as Chloe's sister walked into the room to join m. No, not walked. It was more like a red carpet glide. How ictly did unexceptional Chloe feel about having this beau-l exotic creature for a sister? All Rory's sympathies were th Chloe. The sisters couldn't have looked less alike. He ped Chloe wasn't jealous. Jealousy was a hell of a thing to il around.

In a split second his dazzlement turned to an intense riness and even a lick of sexual antagonism that appeared t of nowhere. It wasn't admirable and it stunned him. He sn't usually *this* judgemental.

She was a redhead. Not Titian. A much deeper shade. More lustrous red one saw in the heart of a garnet, a stone he alled had been sacred to ancient civilisations such as the tecs and the Mayans. She wore her hair long and flowing.

He liked that. Most men would. It curved away from her
and fell over her shoulders like a shining cape. It even li
most glamorously in the evening breeze that wafted thro
the French doors. Her eyes were a jewelled topaz-blue, s
a thick fringe of dark lashes. Her skin wasn't the pale po
lain usually seen in redheads. It had an alluring tint of g
Very very *smooth*. Probably she dyed her hair. That w
explain the skin tones. Her hair was an extraordinary co

She was much taller than Chloe with a body as slender
pliant as a lily. Her yellow silk dress was perfectly simple
to him it oozed style. He might have been staring at s
beautiful young woman who modelled high couture clo
for a living or something equally frivolous like spinning
wheel on a quiz show.

'You know everyone except Rory,' Caroline was say
happy to make the introduction. 'Allegra this is Rory Com
who hails from the Channel Country. Rory, this is Ch
sister, Allegra Hamilton.'

She was walking towards him, graciously extending a
delicate hand. What was he supposed to do, fall to one k
Kiss the air above her fingers? Powerful attraction often
along with a rush of contrary emotions, or so he had r
'How do you do,' she said in that husky voice, as the
equally struck by something in him she didn't quite un
stand, or for that matter *like*.

It might have been a gale force wind instead of a br
blowing through the open doors. Rory swallowed hard o
roaring in his ears. What the hell! One could shake hands
a vision. Get it over. Life went on. He knew he hadn't imag
the shiver of electricity. It was a wonder they hadn't struck s
off one another. It happened. But there was bound to be a s
tific explanation. He felt more comfortable with that, thoug
hadn't the slightest doubt she could cause such a response at

Well ma'am, I survived it!

She didn't smile at him, coolly summing him up. He didn't smile at her. Instead they studied one another with an absolute thoroughness that seemed to lock out everyone else in the room.

She looked away first.

He didn't know how to interpret that. A win or a loss?

Over dinner, it turned out stunning Allegra was also smart. Pretty soon he'd be lost in admiration. Lighthearted conversation set the tone for most of the meal. They talked about anything and everything. A recent art auction, remarkable for the high prices paid for aboriginal art, music, classical and pop, favourite films, books, celebrities in the news, steering clear of anything confrontational. He liked the way she entered spiritedly into the discussions, revealing not only a broad general knowledge, but a wicked sense of humour. Now why should that surprise him? Rory had to chide himself for being so damned chauvinistic in the face of the twenty-first century. Why shouldn't there be a good brain behind that beautiful exterior? His mother had been a clever woman, well educated, well read. Not much of a mother, however, as it turned out. Not all glorious looking women kept themselves busy luring rich guys into marriage he reminded himself.

What *really* struck him, was the way sweet little Chloe kept heckling her sister just about every time she opened her mouth. Heckling was the only way he could interpret it. It was all done with a cutesy smile, which he thought rather odd, but towards the end he found himself fed up with it. Sisterly ease and friendliness appeared to be a thin veneer.

On the other hand—further surprising him—there appeared to be no limit to Allegra's tolerance. She had such a high mettled look to her and surely a redhead's temper he had expected a free-for-all. If again that gorgeous mane was natural? But never once did she retaliate to her sister's running interference when Rory had thought of a few sharp answers himself. There was no way Chloe could be totally free of jealousy, he reasoned. Poor Chloe. This was one of the ways she handled it.

'And what's your feeling, Rory?' Allegra startled him by addressing him directly. She looked across the gleaming table, her beauty quite electrifying amid the candlelight and flowers.

'I'm sorry, I missed that.' *I was too damned busy wondering about you!*

She smiled as though aware of it. 'We were talking about the mystery resignation.' She named a well-known politician who had stunned everyone including the prime minister by vacating his federal seat literally overnight.

'He's had a breakdown, I'd say,' Rory offered quietly, after a moment of reflection.

'Doesn't look like that to me.' Greg Stapleton's mouth curled into a sardonic grin. 'Could be woman trouble. The man looks great, fit and well. I saw him only recently on a talk show. He's a good-looking bloke, happily married supposedly. One of the top performers in government.'

'A high achiever,' Rory agreed. 'And he *is* happily married, with three children. He is a man who drives himself hard. When depression hits it hits hard. It can hit anyone. I've met the man and really admired him.'

'So you think all the stress that goes along with the job—the lengthy periods away from home—got to him?' Allegra asked, studying Rory very carefully and obviously waiting on his answer.

'That's my opinion,' he said. 'But I'm prepared to bet he is the man to confront it and win out.'

She gave a gratifying nod of approval. 'I'm sure we all wish him well.'

Chloe at this point, not to be outdone, attempted to start a rousing political discussion, which was met not so much with disinterest but a disinclination to spoil the mood. Subdued she turned her attention back to cutting down her sister at the same time keeping her own brain underwraps. Appearances could be very deceptive Rory was fast learning. He'd initially thought sweet Chloe would make some man a good wife. Perhaps she *would*. Just so long as her sister wasn't around.

Irritations aside, dinner went off very well. A roulade of salmon with a crab cream sauce; smoked duck breast as a change from beef, a lime and ginger brulée. Someone took an excellent approach to cooking. He hadn't been eating well on the road. Clay and his beautiful wife were the best of hosts; the formal dining room recently redecorated and refurbished was splendid and the food and wine matched up.

It was well after midnight before they broke up. Rory was one of the last to make his way upstairs to his guest room because he and Clay had a private conversation first.

'If you want I could have a word with Allegra in the morning,' Clay suggested, drawing Rory into the book filled library. 'There's a possibility the Sanders property—it's called Naroom by the way—could come on the market.'

'You think they're serious?' Rory asked, staggered by all the leatherbound tomes. Did anyone read them?

'We won't exactly know until I broach the subject.'

'Why Allegra, why not both sisters?' Rory asked, fairly cautiously.

Clay's response was dry. 'Not to be unkind, you've met both sisters. Allegra is definitely the brains of the outfit.'

'Is that why Chloe's so darned resentful?' Rory's chiselled mouth twisted.

'I've never seen Chloe quite so bad,' Clay confessed. '*You* might have had something to do with that!' A teasing grin split his face.

'Cut it out!' Rory's voice was wry. 'I'm sure Chloe can be a very nice person when she tries, but I have to say I'm not interested.'

'What about Allegra?' Clay continued, tongue-in-cheek. 'She's so much more beautiful—'

'And brainier,' Rory cut in. 'Sorry, I know what a beautiful woman can do to a man. You're one of the lucky ones.'

'About as lucky as a man can get,' Clay admitted with a smile. 'Anyway, who could blame Chloe for being so miffed. Allegra has so much going for her.'

'Really?' Rory raised a brow. 'I thought she'd just come out of an unpleasant divorce?'

'So she has. I think she's been feeling a bit down lately. Who could blame her?'

'That must account for the way she hasn't got around to telling her little sister to back off?'

'It's all about sibling rivalry, my man!' Clay groaned. 'Anyway if you like I'll suss out the situation for you in the morning. No harm done one way or the other, but I'm pretty sure they'll want to sell. I'll see what Allegra has to say and let you know.'

'That'll be great, Clay. I much appreciate what you're doing for me and thank you again for your splendid hospitality.'

'A pleasure!' Clay's smile was wide and genuine.

Afterwards Rory found himself following the lingerers Allegra and Chloe up the grand staircase quite unable to prevent himself from admiring Allegra's long slender legs and delicate ankles. Never in his wildest dreams had he anticipated meeting a woman like this. To try to do something about it would be madness. He was a man looking for suitable woman to make his wife. He'd be a total fool to lift his eyes to a goddess who found mortal men dull in a very short time.

He was so engrossed in his thoughts, half admiration, half remonstration, when he almost barged into her. As surefooted as a gazelle, she suddenly stumbled, throwing out a slender ringless hand he had already observed over dinner, to clutch at the banister.

'Oh heavens!' she gasped, sounding relieved he had broken her fall.

'Okay?' Rory's arm shot out like lightning. With his arm around her, his whole body went electric with tension. He dared not even open his mouth again. Instead he stared into her disturbingly beautiful face, unaware his eyes had gone as brilliant and hard as any diamonds.

'She's sloshed!' Chloe explained, looking at her sister aghast.

Rory found himself jumping to Allegra's defence. 'Nothing like it!' His answer came out a shade too curtly, causing poor Chloe to colour up. Allegra Hamilton had had no more than three glasses of wine over the space of the whole evening. He knew that for a fact. He'd rarely taken his eyes off her, which could only mean he had more need of caution.

As it was, he held her lightly but very carefully, surprised the silk dress she wore wasn't going up in smoke. He was searingly aware of the pliant curves and contours of her body. He could smell her perfume. A man could ruin himself over a woman like this. He fully understood that. He just bet she haunted the ex-husband's dreams, poor devil!

'Do you feel faint?' he asked, studying her pale oval face.

Chloe looked on speechlessly.

For a moment Allegra's dazzling gaze locked on his, then when she couldn't hold his gaze any longer, she shook her head as if in an effort to clear it. 'Just a little. It will pass.'

'She doesn't eat,' Chloe informed him like it was an ill kept secret. Her face and neck were flushed with colour. 'Anorexia, you know. Or near enough. So she can wear all those tight clothes.'

Now that just *could* be right, Rory thought. She had eaten lightly at dinner. She was as willowy as a reed. He should know. He still had his arm around her. It felt incredibly, dangerously *intimate*. Anyone would think he'd never had his arm around a woman in his life. He was no monk. But he was, he realised to his extreme discomfort, consumed by the warmth of this woman's body and the lovely fragrance it gave off. It blurred his objective faculties, casting a subversive spell. Allegra Hamilton was a heartbreaker. He knew all about *those*.

'Lord, Chloe, will you stop making it up as you go along. I'm *not* anorexic,' Allegra sighed. 'Though I confess I haven't had much appetite of late. Or much sleep. Thank you, Rory, I'm fine now.' It was said with the faintest trace of acid as though she was aware of the erotic thoughts that were running through his head. She shook back her hair, squared her shoulders and slowly straightened up. 'It was just a fuzzy moment. Nothing to get alarmed about.'

'How many times have I heard you say that after a dinner party?' Chloe directed a tight conspiratorial smile in Rory's direction.

'The fact is you've *never* heard it, Chloe,' Allegra answered with a kind of weary resignation.

'I have, too,' Chloe suddenly barked. 'Mark was real worried about your drinking.'

Allegra laughed shakily. 'What, Diet Coke?'

'Why don't I just carry you to your room?' Rory suggested, not at all happy with the way she was near dragging herself up the stairs, one hand on the banister. He didn't wa

o hear about her ex-husband, either. Not tonight anyway.
You'd be as light as a feather.'

'You're kidding!' She paused to give him a vaguely
aunting glance. 'A feather?'

'If I pick you up I can prove it. You look to me like you need
arrying to your room.' Before she could say another word or
get out a word of protest, he scooped her up in his arms.

'There, what did I tell you?' His voice mocked her, but in
eality he was seized by a feeling of intoxication that was
enormously distracting. It came at him in mounting waves.
For one forbidden moment he went hot with desire, quite
vithout the power to cool it. Never before had a woman stirred
uch a response. His every other experience paled into insig-
ificance beside this. A man of good sense should fear such
nings as not all that long ago men feared witches.

She caught her breath, astounded by his action. Then she
ave way to laughter. 'A woman has to be careful around you
can see, Rory Compton. I've never been swept off my feet
efore. Though it does fit your image.'

'What image?' He looked down at her with his brooding,
ght filled eyes.

'Man of action. It's written all over you.'

'Look I'm really sorry, Rory,' Chloe said, trotting in
eir wake. 'Allegra is always doing things like this. It's so
nbarrassing.'

'Give me a break, Chloe!' Allegra broke into a moan
efore she was overcome again by laughter. Peals of it. It
nply took her over. 'I've never met a man like Rhett Butler
efore,' she gasped.

Though her mood seemed lighthearted, Rory had the odd
eling she was on the verge of tears. A woman's tears could
nder a man very vulnerable. He knew when she was alone
her room they might flow.

With his arms around her body, her beautiful face so clos
excitement was pouring into him way beyond the level
comfort. Wariness had turned to wonder. Wonder to a da
albeit *involuntary* desire. She might have been naked in l
arms so acutely did his senses respond.

Oh ye of little resolve! A taunting voice started up in his hea
But then he hadn't seen a woman like Allegra Hamilton comi

What he needed now was a long, cold bracing shower. S
was an incredibly desirable woman yet he was half appalled
his own reactions, the depth and dimension, the sheer physi
pleasure he took in holding her. The breasts he couldn't help b
look down on, were small but beautifully shaped; her should
delicately feminine. Her arched neck had the elegance o
swan's. What would a man feel like carrying a woman such
this to their bridal bed? It came to him with a fierce jolt he deep
resented the fact another man had already done so. How co
that same man bring himself to let her go? He didn't really kn
but he was prepared to bet it was she who had tossed her husba
aside. And how many other men had she ensnared before hi

It was more than time to set her down before she tota
messed him up.

Chloe ran ahead helpfully and opened the bedroom do
'Anyone would think she was a baby. She can walk.' S
looked up at Rory sympathetically. 'Just put her on the be

My God, didn't he want to!

He was no damned different from all the other poor foo
Whatever his mind said, whatever his will demanded, und
neath he was just a man whose fate was to succumb to wom

'Please, Chloe,' Allegra laughed. 'I'm the wronged par
It's this cowboy who swept me off my feet.'

'Cattleman, ma'am,' he corrected, now so pervers
hostile he barely stopped himself from pitching her onto
huge four-poster bed, its timber glowing honey-gold.

'Rory, I didn't mean to offend you,' she apologised, still caught between laughter and tears.

'Forgive me, I think you did.' He couldn't say he badly resented being put under a spell. He wasn't accustomed to such things.

'I confess I find *your* attitude a little worrying, too.' From a lying position—God how erotic—she sat up on the bed, staring at him with her great topaz-blue eyes.

'Hey, what on earth are you two talking about?' Chloe was struggling hard to keep up. It all seemed incomprehensible to her.

'Nothing. Absolutely nothing,' Rory said, further perplexing her. Allegra Hamilton in the space of one evening had got right under his skin. He was aware his muscles had gone rigid with the effort not to yield to the urge to lean forward, close the space between them, grasp those delicate shoulders and kiss her hard. Only desiring a woman like that was an option he simply couldn't afford.

Maybe it was her utter unattainability that made her so desirable to him? He had to find a reason to give him comfort. On his way to the door Rory turned to give her one last glance.

A big mistake!

She couldn't have looked more ravishing or the setting more marvellously appropriate. The quilted bedspread gleamed an opulent gold, embroidered with richly coloured flowers. Her dress had ridden up over her lovely legs, pooling around her in deep yellow. Her hair shone a rich red beneath an antique gilt and crystal chandelier that hung from a central rose in the plastered ceiling. Hanging over the head of the bed was a very beautiful flower painting of yellow roses in a brass bowl, lit from above.

It was enough to steal any man's breath away.

'Good night, Rory,' she said sweetly, which he translated into, 'Goodbye!'

He nodded his dark head curtly, but made no response.

Witch!

She was accustomed to putting men under a spell. But for all he knew she could have a heart of ice.

Coming as he did from the desert where there was a much higher pitch of light and the vast landscape was so brilliantly coloured, Rory found his trip out to Naroom, enjoyable, but relatively uninspiring compared to his own region, the Channel Country. The bones of many dead men lay beneath the fiery iron-oxide red soil of his nearly eight hundred thousand square kilometre desert domain. The explorers Burke and Wills had perished there; the great Charles Sturt, the first explorer to ever enter the Simpson Desert almost came to final grief—the German Ludwig Leichhardt became a victim of the forbidding landscape. Not only had the early explorers been challenged by that wild land, but so too were the pioneering cattlemen like his forebears who had followed. After good rains, the best cattle fattening country in the world, in times of drought they had to exploit the water in the Great Artesian Basin, which lay beneath the Simpson Desert to keep their vast herds alive. And exploitation was the word. It really worried him that one day the flow of water to the several natural springs and the artificial bores might cease. What a calamity!

To Rory, the desert atmosphere of home was so vivid he could smell it and taste it on his tongue. These vast central plains seemed much nearer civilisation. He had lived all his life in a riverine desert, bordered on Turrawin's west by the one hundred thousand square kilometre Simpson Desert of central Australia. His world was a world of infinite horizons and maybe because of it, the desert possessed an extraordinary mystique.

It was certainly a different world from the silvery plains he was driving through. His landscapes were surreal. They seeped into a man's soul. The desert was where he belonged, he thought sadly, though he accepted it was fearsome country compared to those gentler, more tranquil landscapes; the silvers, the browns, the dark sapphires and the sage-greens. He was used to a sun scorched land where the shifting red sands were decorated with bright golden clumps of Spinifex that glowed at dusk. Scenically the Channel Country was not duplicated by any other region on the continent. It was unique.

Unique, too, the way the desert, universally a bold fiery-red, was literally smothered in wildflowers of all colours after the rains. No matter what ailed him such sights had always offered him relief, a safety valve after grim exchanges with his father, even a considerable degree of healing. There were just some places one *belonged*. Fate had made him a second son and given him a father who had shown himself to be without heart. He was the second son who was neither wanted nor needed.

Well let it lie.

Clay as promised had set up this meeting with the Sanders women. Clay would have come along, only he was fathoms deep in work. Rory would have liked his company—they got on extremely well together—but he didn't mind. It was just the two sisters and their mother. An exploratory chat. Just the two sisters? Who was he kidding? He couldn't wait to lay eyes on Allegra Hamilton again. In fact it hadn't been easy putting her out of his mind.

You can handle it, he told himself.

With no conviction whatever.

Clay had assured him Mrs Sanders *was* seriously consider-ing selling, although the property wasn't on the market as yet.

Clay, during his conversation with the beauteous Mrs Hamilton, had formed the idea the family would want between $3.5 and $4 million, although she hadn't given much away. Clay got the impression Allegra didn't really want to sell.

Why not? It wasn't as though a woman like that, a hothouse orchid, could work the place. Nevertheless Rory had already taken the opportunity of having a long, private phone conversation with one of Turrawin's bankers. A man he was used to and who knew him and his capabilities. He had been given the go-ahead on a sizeable loan to match his own equity. Naroom wasn't a big property as properties in his part of the world went—nowhere near the size of Jimboorie for that matter, let alone Turrawin. The property from all accounts had been allowed to run down following the death of Llew Sanders and the unexpected departure of their overseer who it was rumoured had had a falling out with Mrs Sanders. A woman who 'kept herself to herself' and consequently wasn't much liked. Rory wanted to ask where Allegra had got her extraordinary looks from, but thought it unfair to Chloe who seemed a nice little thing if she could just hurdle the sibling rivalry or trade in her present life for a new one.

Rivalry simply hadn't existed between him and Jay. They had always been the best of friends. The strong bond formed in early childhood had only grown closer with the changing circumstances of their lives. In many ways he had taken on the mantle of older brother even though he was two years Jay's junior. He had shielded the quieter, more sensitive Jay through their traumatic adolescence and gone on to take the burden away from Jay in the running of the station. That old hypocrite, his father, had been well aware of it but chose—because it suited him—to keep his mouth and his purse shut.

Valerie Sanders walked into the kitchen in time to see Allegra taking a tray of chocolate chip cookies out of the ven, presumably to offer to their visitor with tea or coffee. ooking wasn't Valerie's forte so she had left Allegra to it. esides she had sacked their housekeeper, Beth, who didn't now how to keep a still tongue in her head, even after ourteen years.

'I hope you're not going to be difficult, Allegra,' Valerie, a im and attractive fifty-two-year-old now said, picking up eir discussion from breakfast. 'I want the place sold. So does hloe. Why should you care? You don't live here. You have stop thinking of yourself for a change.'

Allegra transferred the cookies to a wire cooling rack fore answering. She had learned long ago to ignore Valerie's rennial sniping. Crossing swords with her only reinforced . 'That's a bit unfair, Val,' she said mildly. 'All I said was, e can't simply *give* Naroom away. It's worth every penny of 4 million even if it's not the best of times to sell. Dad would rn over in his grave if we sold it for less. It just seemed to e you and Chloe are prepared to accept the first offer.'

Valerie's light blue gaze turned baleful. 'I want *out*, llegra. I've had more than enough of life on the land and hloe has had *no* life at all. I know you don't worry about your ster. But she has to find a good man to marry and she isn't etting any younger. You had a good man and you were fool ough to let him get away.'

Allegra refused to fire. 'Do you actually listen to a word I y, Val? Mark was unfaithful to me. Since when are philan- rers good men?' She busied herself setting out cups and ucers. 'As for Chloe, I used to invite her to stay with us often ough. Surely you remember?'

'How could she stay when there was always tension tween you and Mark?' Valerie retaliated. 'Though it must said Mark always did his best to pretend nothing was rong. Chloe and I have come to the conclusion *you* were the

source of all the trouble, Allegra, however much you prote
And you've always gone out of your way to put your sister
the shade. You could have been a real help to her, but you li
in your own little world.'

Allegra couldn't help a groan escaping her. 'So you'
been pointing out to me for years and years. Now we're
the subject of Chloe, she's not much help around the place
hear her complaining about putting on weight when t
surefire answer is exercise. There's plenty to do around t
house since you let Beth go.'

'We couldn't afford her,' Valerie said briefly.

'She been with us for years and years,' Allegra sa
thankful she had managed to contact Beth who was now livi
with her sister

'That awful woman!' Beth, her anger up, had raged.
only stayed because of your dad. It was all so different wh
you left home, Ally love. Personally I think your stepmotl
drove your poor dear father bonkers! He must have spe
years of his life wondering why he married her.'

He married her for my sake, Allegra thought sadly. To gi
me a mother.

'Now when this young man arrives I want you to stay
the background,' Valerie said. ' If such a thing is possible. Yo
father spoilt you terribly.'

'I suppose he was trying to make up for you, Val,' Alleg
offered dryly. 'I've always irritated the living daylights out
you.' In fact Allegra couldn't recall a happy, carefree peri
of her life; a time when she was not exposed to Valeri
shrouded antagonism, which nevertheless Allegra was ma
aware of even as a child.

'So you have,' Valerie admitted. 'You must have irritat
the living daylights out of Mark as well. You could have he
onto him with a little understanding. We all know men are

e habit of having a bit on the side But your ego couldn't
lerate that, could it?'

Allegra considered this, aghast. 'My ego had nothing to do
ith it. Dad didn't have a bit on the side as you phrase it.'

'No, he was faithful to the memory of your sainted
other!' At long last Valerie gave vent to the helpless anger
e'd been forced to stifle for years; anger that had at its heart
alousy of a ghost.

'Now you've come out with it.' Allegra experienced a hard
ng. 'I can see from now on it's going to be no-holds-barred.
hat's the answer to all our woes, isn't it? I'm guilty of re-
mbling my mother who died before she was thirty. Think
out that, Val. You're *jealous* of a woman who died so
ung? Would you have swapped places with her? It's truly
d, but you've never been able to master your deep envy of
r place in Dad's life. The fact I look so much like her has
ly made you fixate on it all these long years. I suppose it
as inevitable.'

'Psychoanalyst now are we?' Valerie jeered, her expression
tter. 'Actually I'm fine. Llew is dead. Naroom will soon be
ld. It was never really *my* home. More *her* shrine. No need
r us to put up a pretence anymore. But don't kid yourself.
e conflicts we've had over the years have been caused by
ur pushing me or your sister to the limit. I wasn't your
rling mummy. You were such an assertive child, always de-
anding your father's attention. You took your demands to
e next stage with your husband. Small wonder he left you.'

'Oh go jump, Val!' Allegra had come to the end of her
ther. '*I* left Mark. But don't let's upset your mind-set.'

'Mark told me *you* made him feel alienated,' Valerie per-
sted.

'Since when did you become Mark's champion?' Allegra
ked wearily. 'He's ancient history, Val.'

The expression on Valerie's face was one of primitive [an]tagonism. 'Alienation was the cause of much of his unhap[pi]ness and his turning to someone else.'

Allegra groaned with frustration. 'You're talking throu[gh] your hat. It was more than some*one* else, Val.'

'I bet you had your little flings as well,' Valerie quic[kly] countered. 'You demand constant admiration.'

'None of which has ever been handed out by you. So[me] stepmothers are wonderful. Heaps of them! But y[our] crowning achievement has been picking on me. All your l[ove] has been given to your own child. I had to lean heavily on D[ad.] You set out early to drive a wedge between me and Chloe. Y[ou] bred your own resentment into her. As for my marriage, I [re]spected my vows.'

Valerie gave a mocking smile. 'The reason I underst[and] exactly what Mark meant when he said you alienated hi[m] because you alienate *me*.'

'Then I'm sorry!' Allegra threw up her hands, thinking [a] stepmother's problems with her would never be resolved u[ntil] the family—such as it was—split up. Her father had h[eld] them all together. Now he was gone. 'I have to get chang[ed,]' she said, moving towards the door. 'Rory Compton shoul[d be] here soon.'

'Set to fascinate him, are we?' Valerie called after her.

The facade of caring stepmother was rapidly crumbli[ng.]

In her bedroom Allegra changed out of the loose dress sh[e'd] been wearing since breakfast into a cool top with a gypsy s[tyle] skirt that created a breeze around her legs. She slung a si[lver]studded belt around her narrow waist and hunted up a pai[r of] turquoise sandals to match her outfit. It was second natur[e to] her to try to look her best no matter how she felt. For one th[ing] her job as Fashion Editor on a glossy magazine demande[d]

Besides, looking good gave her the extra confidence she needed. It helped her present her best face to the world.

Inside, these days, she felt totally derailed. Her beloved father gone. The only person in the world who had truly loved her. Val coming out into the open, spitting chips! No husband to be there for her. What does a woman do when she can't keep her husband of three years faithful? So much for beauty! She had thought in her naivete, she and Mark would be together for life—Mark the father of her children—but she and Mark had been marching to a very different tune. Fidelity simply wasn't in his nature, though he had given every outward semblance of it for quite a while. That was until she received in the mail a batch of photographs, stunning evidence of her husband's betrayal. They were sent anonymously of course. Not a single word accompanied them as though the photographs said it all; which indeed they did. They were from someone who didn't so much care about her pain as showing Mark up for what he was. Allegra had always had the idea that person was a woman. Someone who may have been a former lover of Mark's and now hated him.

Mark's explanation when she had confronted him with them had been quite extraordinary. He had acted calm, as though he couldn't quite grasp her devastating shock.

'It's long over, Ally!' He'd assured her in his smooth, convincing stockbroker's voice. 'It meant absolutely nothing. All I did was relieve a physical ache at the time. Let's face it, my darling, I don't get as much sex from you, as I want, though I have to admit it increases your allure. Why do women make such a big deal about men having extra needs? It's *you* I love. You're my *wife*. No other woman can touch you. I'll never leave you and you'll never leave me. I'd be devastated if you did.'

She was the one who was devastated but, God help her, she had forgiven him. It was too early in their marriage to call it a day. She certainly couldn't go home to Val to seek advice and comfort. She told herself lots of people make mistakes. She made herself believe it had been Mark's only infidelity. In retrospect, of course it hadn't been. Mark was addicted to sex like another man might have been addicted to golf. It was a necessary relaxation, a *fix*. Mark was handsome, charming, successful, generous. Especially with his favours.

In the beginning he had been a tender, sensitive, romantic lover, eager to please her. She realised now what he had been doing was gradually trying to break her in to his little ways she found vaguely demeaning, though she tried to understand where he was coming from. It wasn't as though there was much harm in what he wanted her to do it. It wasn't even over-poweringly sensual. But she couldn't help feeling titillating little games were ridiculous. Certainly they didn't turn her on.

'Sweetheart, you're not a bit of fun!'

Seeing how she felt, he backed off. Overnight he rectified his behaviour, which had never been evident during their courtship, returning to the considerate, caring lover. She'd believed like a fool they had come to an understanding. Nothing further was going to be allowed to disrupt their lives. Only Mark secretly moved back to the kind of women who were up for the kind of sexual kicks he craved. The other women turned out to be married women from their own circle. Why had she been so shocked? Faithless friends made faithless lovers. All of them had been exceedingly careful, not wanting exposure or even to break up their existing marriages. There was no wild partying, no staying out overnight much less for long weekends. Their marriage might have survived for quite a bit longer only she had returned home from work unexpectedly early one afternoon only to find Mark and a married friend of theirs chasing one another around the bedroom.

Incredibly she hadn't been laid low. She hadn't screamed or cried or yelled at the woman to get dressed and get the hell out of her house. For a moment she had very nearly laughed. They looked so ridiculous staring back at her. Like a pair of startled kangaroos caught in the headlights of a four-wheel drive.

'Goodness, Penny, I scarcely recognised you without your clothes!'

Then she had turned about and walked straight out of the house, booking into a hotel.

So here she was at twenty-seven, a betrayed wife. A betrayed ex-wife. And having a hard time coming to terms with what a fool she had been. She had truly believed Mark was a man of integrity. Yet love or what she thought had been love had flown out the window. Indeed it had all but taken wing when she had first received those compromising photographs with her clever handsome husband caught in the act, his unflattering position preventing her from seeing his partner-in-crime's face. At one stage, as she bent over the photographs, she had the weirdest notion that partner could have been Chloe—something about the slight plumpness of the legs, what she could see of the woman's body?—but quickly rejected the idea, disgusted with herself for even allowing such a notion to cross her mind. Chloe would never do such a thing. Chloe was far too honourable.

Incredibly Mark had tried desperately to save their marriage, saying she was making something out of nothing. Just how did one define *nothing*? A man wasn't intended to remain monogamous, he said. Everyone knew that. Smart women accepted it; turned a blind eye.

He obviously didn't want to consider the innumerable crimes of passion that hit the headlines. He continued to hold to the line he 'adored' her. He knew he had a problem of sorts, but he would seek counselling if that's what she wanted. They would go together.

She had declined without regrets. She had to face the dismal fact Mark was highly unlikely to be cured. Sooner or later he would break out again. He had found it ridiculously easy up to date. Almost ten years her senior and well versed in the less laudable ways of the world, he had run rings around her. Even after their divorce became final he had stalked her, telling her how ashamed he was of his behaviour and how much he desperately needed her. Didn't he deserve another chance?

Tell me. Whatever it is you want me to do, I'll do it. I've already entered into treatment.

She knew it was a lie. The only thing Mark was sorry about was getting *caught*.

Why had she married him in the first place? He hadn't exactly swept her off her feet, though he couldn't have been kinder, sweeter, or more considerate. His intellect had reached out to her. He was a clever, cultured man, highly successful with powerful friends. She went from single woman with no *real* home—home with Valerie and had felt like enemy territory—to married woman with a beautiful home of her own and an extraordinarily generous husband who showered her with gifts. Was that what she had really wanted all along?

A home of her own?

She never told anyone about Mark's little idiosyncrasies. She could well be confiding in someone who already knew. She didn't blacken his name. She knew quite a few in their circle believed she was the one to bring what had appeared to be a marriage made in heaven to an abrupt end. Mark was 'a lovely guy!' Everyone knew he adored her. The age difference might have had something to do with it. Or Allegra had found someone else. In her work she was invited everywhere with or without her husband—there had to be lots of temptations along the way, men and women behaving the way they did.

Allegra knew people had been talking, but there was little she could do about it but take it on the chin.

CHAPTER THREE

RORY COMPTON had already arrived by the time she made her
way downstairs. She realized with a prickle of something like
discomfort and an irrational guilt she had taken a few extra
little pains with her appearance. She was aware too of a quick-
ening of excitement that was gathering in strength. She hadn't
expected anything like it. Not here, not *now*. Not when she
wanted time to re-evaluate her life. She was a woman trying
to recover from a recent divorce. Sad things had happened to
her, leaving her feeling low, but the advent of Rory Compton
into her life had sparked off some sort of revival. Without
wanting to, or without planning it, he had somehow brought
her back to life. Could it possibly have something to do with
the rebound syndrome? She had actually seen it at work with
a friend. Women were very vulnerable after the break-up of
a relationship. Was she one of them?

Since she had met him she had started to ask herself that
very question. She couldn't stop thinking of him though she
had willed herself not to. But like all things forbidden he had
stuck in her mind. There was just something about the man
that had penetrated the miasma of grief she had been battling
since the death of her beloved father and the failure of her
marriage. She had been certain in her mind she wanted to

emain untouchable. At least for a proper period of time. In a ense she was mourning the death of her marriage; the death f a dream.

Rory Compton had changed all that and in a remarkably hort space of time. She would do well to see the danger in hat. All it had needed was a glance from his remarkable eyes; he peculiar excitement she had felt when he had swept her p into his arms; the way her heart rate had speeded up. He ad drawn from her not only a physical, but an emotional esponse. It wasn't simply his arresting looks. She had really ked the way he had been at the Cunningham's dinner party; is sense of humour, his broad range of interests and the ympathy and sensitivity he had shown towards the politician, fellow man battling the depression that had fallen on him o unexpectedly.

Rory Compton was formidable, she had concluded. A real resence for a man his age. There was something very pur- oseful and intent about him and she had to concede a hidden nger, or at the very least brooding. He had actually made her eel like her old self. Correction. More like she was running t full throttle. Was it the adversarial look in those silver rosted eyes? Or the taunting half smile? He was physically ery strong. He had lifted her as though she weighed no more an a twelve-year-old. She sensed his physical attraction to er—given that it was quite involuntary—maddened him. Iere was a man who liked to be in control.

Holding her in his arms had quite spoilt it for him. The truth vas—she couldn't hide it from herself—she had been as roused as he was. Powerful physical attraction was a aunting thing, especially when it came out of left field. She vould do well to be wary of it. Once bitten, twice shy? What id she know of him after all? Her judgement had been way ff with Mark. She wasn't about to make a habit of it. She needed to know much more about Rory Compton. It would be better given her background to mistrust rather than trust.

What you're feeling, girl, are hormones. You have to let it pass.

He was seated on the verandah at the white wicker table, Valerie and Chloe flanked him, both looking surprisingly mellow. Chloe too had gone to some pains, Allegra thought gently. Her apple blossom skin that flushed easily heightened the colour of her eyes and she was wearing a very pretty dress Allegra had brought with her as a present, knowing exactly what would best suit her sister.

Allegra paused for a moment in the open doorway, hoping she had given them enough time alone with their visitor as requested, though requested was too polite a word.

Immediately Rory Compton saw her he sprang to his feet, the man of dark compelling looks she too vividly remembered. A wedge of crow-black hair had fallen forwards on his forehead giving him a very attractive, slightly rakish look. Worn longer than was usual, his glossy, thick textured hair curled up at his nape. It would be great hair to touch. His eyes glittered against his bronze skin. Today his cheekbones looked more pronounced. There wasn't a skerrick of weight on him. His nose was very straight above his beautifully cut mouth. Not generously full lipped like Mark's, but firm and chiselled. He had the sort of face one wouldn't forget in a hurry.

Despite her little pep talks to herself she forgot about betrayal, failure and the tense situation that existed between her and Valerie. She pretended she was considering a particularly sexy man to act as the foil for the beautiful female model in a fashion shoot. No question he would get the job. Two or three inches over six feet, by and large he was moving from lean to nearly thin even in the couple of days since she had last seen him. It startled her to realise it, but something about

im caught at her heart. It was a sentiment that in its tender-
ess took her completely by surprise. This man was eating
vay at her defences. No wonder she felt a tingle of alarm.

As on the first occasion when they had been introduced,
e didn't smile and he had a wonderful smile. She'd seen it
rected at Chloe among others. She didn't smile, either, and
ere was nothing wrong with *her* smile. Instead she inclined
r head in acknowledgement of his presence. Both of them
atched up in self-protectiveness, she thought. Perversely
e wondered as her eyes alighted on his mouth what it would
e like to kiss those chiselled lips?

Don't think about it!

She had nothing to hope for with Rory Compton. He was
near stranger It was the wrong time for starting another re-
tionship anyway, though she couldn't help but be aware
ere was *something* between them.

'Mrs Hamilton!' He inclined his dark head in greeting.

'Please, Allegra.' It came out more coolly than she
tended. She planned to drop the Hamilton anyway.

'Well now we'd almost given up on you!' Val announced,
though Allegra was habitually late and consciously rude.

'Why is that, Val?'

Rory held a chair for her. He hadn't been expecting to hear
r call her mother by her Christian name, or to mark the
virling undercurrents now they were together. This wasn't
e close-knit family, he swiftly intuited. Chloe had no
oblem with 'Mum.' In fact Chloe was sweetly affectionate
wards her mother and her mother clearly doted on her. That
asn't the case, it seemed, with her elder daughter.

'Well you did tell us you had plenty of other things to do,'
hloe started into a deliberate lie. Why did men have to look
Allegra the way they did? It brought out the worst in her.

'Like making coffee or tea?' Allegra looked down on her

sister's silky brown head. 'Would you like to come and help me?' *Since when?* When there was a job to be done it had never taken Chloe long to disappear. Born and reared on a working station Chloe had no love of the outdoor life or work of any kind. As a girl she had always wanted to stay at home with Mum who had never encouraged Chloe to pull her weight.

Valerie, as was her practice, jumped in on Chloe's behalf. 'Chloe has opted to take Rory for a drive around the property. But we would like coffee first. Coffee for you, Rory? Or tea if you prefer?' Valerie smiled at this extraordinarily personable young man. Chloe had already told her how strikingly handsome he was. Not to mention those eyes!

Rory, however, turned to Allegra. She was so damned magnetic he decided there and then caution had to determine his every response. 'Coffee's fine,' he said. 'Sure *I* can't help you bring it out?'

Some imp of mischief got into Allegra. 'Thank you so much,' she said gracefully. 'Please come through.' She turned to lead the way, but not before catching the glare in Valerie's eyes.

Under the terms of her father's will his estate had been split three ways, but not in the way any of them had expected. Certainly not Valerie. She and Chloe had each inherited quarter shares; Allegra half, much to Valerie's outrage.

If I want to invite this man into the house I have a perfect right to do so no matter the scowl on Valerie's face, Allegra thought. Her father's will had further alienated her from her family when she had thought their mutual loss would bring them closer together.

Faint hope! She knew Valerie and Chloe believed she had received a handsome divorce settlement from Mark but she had refused to take a penny. How could she do such a thing? The choice to end the marriage had been hers. She wanted nothing of Mark's, even the beautiful jewellery he had given

er. She hadn't even opted to take her wedding ring let alone
e magnificent solitaire diamond engagement ring. He could
ve that for her successor.

ory followed her into the large well equipped kitchen, definitely
oubled by the undercurrents. He was surprised Allegra—who
oked like she was used to being waited on hand and foot—was
e one to organise the morning tea. He really had to stop being
 quick with his assumptions Blame it on his unnatural bias.

'Coffee, you said?' She gave him a glance that just stopped
ort of challenge.

He understood because he felt the same powerful urge to
allenge her. He didn't understand exactly why, but he did
now everything had changed since he had met her. 'Yes, thank
ou.' He looked about him. 'You have a very attractive home.'

'It actually needs refurbishing,' she said, setting the per-
olator on the hot plate. 'Nothing has been touched since my
other redecorated it in the early days of her marriage.'

That meant well over twenty years surely? Chloe had told
m that first evening she was twenty-three to Allegra's
enty-seven. She had made twenty-seven sound more like
venty-two. 'She hasn't felt the urge to try her hand again?'
 asked. 'I thought women loved rearranging things.'

Allegra sliced into the fruit cake she had made the previous
y. 'So we do, but my mother, sadly, is no longer with us. She
as killed in a car crash when I was a toddler. I would have been
led, too, only it was one of the rare times I wasn't with her.'

Initially he felt shock, then an explanation for the things
at were troubling him. 'I'm very sorry for your loss,' he said
ith sincerity. 'So Valerie is your stepmother?'

'And Chloe my half sister,' she nodded. 'My father remar-
ed when I was three. A lot of people think Val is my mother
cause she's always been there.'

He looked at her keenly. 'But she wasn't the mother yo
wanted?'

She took a few moments to answer. 'You're going to psy
choanalyse me?'

'No, just a question.'

'Why would you *say* that?' She wasn't surprised, howeve
by his perception.

He gave a self-deprecating shrug. 'I'm an authority o
mothers that go missing. Mine left home when I was twelv
and my brother, Jay, fourteen.'

'And the reason, seeing we're cutting right through th
usual preliminaries?'

'She couldn't take it anymore,' he offered bluntly.

'She was having marital problems?' Allegra began to loa
the trolley.

'You would know about them,' he answered in a lo
dark voice.

'Indeed I do,' she returned smartly.

'Yes, she was having problems,' he admitted, thinking th
very air scintillated around her. 'My father was and remai
a very difficult man.'

'You look like you might have a few hang-ups of your own'
She stopped what she was doing and pinned him with her gaz

'Thanks for noticing,' he said suavely.

'Don't feel bad about it. I have them as well. So name one

'I don't trust beautiful women.'

Her stomach did a little flip. He could say that yet it wa
as if he had reached out and kissed her. 'Never in this world'
Somehow she managed a smile.

'No.' Slowly he shook his head, not breaking the eye contac

'Wow!' The expression on her face was both satirical an
amused. 'We're going to have lots to talk about. I don't tru
handsome men.'

'I understood your ex-husband adored you?' Now that was
finitely a challenge.

'We had different ideas about what being 'adored' meant.
hink you actually *did* adore your mother?'

His eyes turned as turbulent as a stormy sea. 'We both did.
y and I. Seen from our point of view her leaving was an
andonment.'

'But you see her now?' she asked, fully expecting the
swer to be yes.

He picked up three lemons and juggled them in his sure
nds. 'Not for many years,' he said and returned the lemons
the bowl. 'Close on fifteen.'

'Good grief!' She didn't hide her surprise. 'So you haven't
en her since you were a boy?' She wondered how that could
ve been allowed to happen.

He held aloof. 'That's right, Mrs Hamilton.' He focused on
tching her move around the kitchen. She was very efficient
her movements. In fact she was perfectly at home in a
chen when he had been too ready to think she was the
intessential hothouse flower who lay about gracefully while
meone else did the work.

'Allegra,' she corrected, speaking sharply because he was
nerving her and he knew it. 'Sorry, I don't care for Mrs
milton,' she said more calmly. 'You don't feel motivated
find her?'

He didn't hesitate. 'No. But I know where she is.'

She had to suck air into her lungs. 'You make it sound like
e outer reaches of the galaxy.'

'Might as well be.' Rory had to steady himself, too, unwill-
g for her to see just how much the old trauma still hurt. 'It's
ong, hard road back from betrayal, *Allegra*.' He placed
cking emphasis on her name.

She studied his handsome, brooding face for a moment.

'Isn't it strange how we punish the ones we love? You're absolutely sure you know the reason? She must have been desperately unhappy?'

He took so long to answer she thought he was going to ignore her question. 'That's there under the abandonment,' he conceded. 'I guess she was unhappy. For a *while* at least.' He put a mocking hand to his heart, his luminous eyes dangerously bright. 'She remarried a couple of years later.'

'Life goes on.' She shrugged. 'So did my dad, but he never forgot my mother. One of the reasons he remarried so soon was that he needed a wife to look after me.'

And what a beautiful child she must have been! Rory let his gaze rest on her, aware his fingers were curled tight into his palms as though he might make some involuntary move towards her. A woman like that any man could lose his senses. But to let himself fall in love with her would be one hell of an ill fated idea. She had wonderful skin, wonderful colouring. He allowed his eyes, at least, to barely skim the low neckline of her top. It dipped as she moved, revealing the satin-smooth upper curves of her breasts. The blue of the clingy little top was the same colour as her eyes. Of course she knew that. She wore her mane of garnet hair in a classic knot. And it *was* natural. Abandoning indifference if only for a moment he had asked Chloe. Chloe said the only nice thing she had said about her sister all night. 'Yes, isn't it beautiful? Hair that colour is rare!'

The sheer power of a beautiful woman!. A lover of beauty in all its forms, Rory felt himself drenched in heat. He had to realise he was achingly vulnerable to this particular woman. A woman like that could take a lot off a man without giving a thing back.

Belatedly he picked up the conversation. 'And that woman was Valerie?'

'Yes.' Allegra for her part, didn't fully understand why the

n moved her like he did. It was as though she could see
ough the layers of defences accumulated through the years,
when he was a handsome, daring little boy. A little boy who
d the capacity to be badly hurt.

'A lot of expectations were put on her,' he said.

'Absolutely!' Her answer was faintly bitter in response to
: irony of his tone.

'It can't be an easy job trying to raise another woman's
ld?' He looked at her, lifting a black brow.

'No one suggested it was,' she said bluntly.

'Okay, I'll back off.'

'Do.' She was frosty in her tone. 'To get off the subject, I
ght as well tell you I've read up on Compton Holdings. I'll
: a few questions of my own now, if I may? Why did you
ve? Surely with a huge enterprise and a flagship station like
crawin there was more than enough room and work for two
others? Or a dozen brothers for that matter.'

His expression hardened. 'For most people there would be,
: you haven't met my father. My father is a very control-
g sort of man and I'm long past marching to his drumbeat.
eeded to strike out on my own.'

'Then you have the money to buy here?' She resorted to a
sk business-like tone.

'Always supposing I'm interested.' His eyes mocked her.
aven't seen over the place yet.'

'You wouldn't be here if you thought it a waste of time,
: I warn you I'm no push-over, Rory Compton.'

'Excuse me, *you* inherited?' He leaned back nonchalantly
inst a cabinet and folded his arms.

What a combination of male graces he had, such an
gance of movement. 'I'm the major shareholder,' she
ormed him coolly, aware of something else. He offered
ment as well as poignancy.

'That's unusual?'

'Well *you'd* know all about that.' She came back spirited

'Touché!' Unexpectedly he gave her his rare smile. It w
so heartbreaking it was just as well it came and went fair
rarely. 'I think we got off on the wrong foot, Allegra.'

She wanted to remain as cool as a cucumber but the w
he said her name tugged at her heart. Perversely it remind
her of the need for caution. How could her interest in a m
reawaken so quickly after her divorce? The answer? This m
was too compelling. 'That happens when people are wary
one another, ' she said.

'*Are* we?' he asked , feigning a wondering voice. Neith
of them could deny there was a strong current runni
between them.

'Isn't that the word you would use?' She kept her eyes
him. No struggle at all.

'As I say, it pays to be wary around a beautiful woma
Impatiently he slicked that troublesome stray lock back. 'L
I mention I find you beautiful?' Well, she knew that for a fa
No harm in getting it out into the open.

'That worries you?' Her blue eyes checked on his expressi

'Terribly.' He smiled.

The really extraordinary thing was she smiled bac
'Whatever looks I have they haven't done me much good,' s
said wryly.

'But I understood from Chloe you're a fashion editor
a magazine? If they wanted someone to look the part y
had to be it.'

'Why thank you, Rory.'

He smiled. 'If I know anything about women, it's they li
to be complimented now and then.'

'True. Okay, my looks were important there,' s
conceded. 'But I wanted a happy marriage far more tha

successful career. I wanted children. I wanted family. I wanted years and years and years of watching my kids grow up. I wanted grandchildren. I wanted my husband and myself to grow old together, still in love.'

He gave her a searching look. 'A lot of wants, Allegra. You didn't try for a family?' God a man would so want a child with her.

There was pain in her expression. 'You don't know when to quit do you? That's a very personal question.'

'Maybe, but I'm in pursuit of truth here. It so happens, I'm looking for a wife.'

Her heart did a somersault in her breast. 'Is that your next career move?' Somehow she gave the question an edge of sarcasm.

'Sure is. Total commitment,' he confirmed.

'Don't dare look at *me*.' She issued the warning with a little laugh. 'I won't be thinking of marriage for a long, long time.'

'Afraid?'

'You bet!' she answered swiftly. 'I made one mistake. I'm sure you'll appreciate I'll be very cautious about making another. To be honest, Rory, I didn't see *your* offer coming.' She gave him a sparkling glance.

'I didn't make one, did I? Hell, I'm as cautious as you, Allegra. But I have to tell you, you impress me.' He made a mock study of her as though she were a possible candidate. 'You're a highly desirable woman in any man's language, but there's that wary bit we both share.'

'Maybe you'd be more in tune with Chloe?' she suggested. 'And here I was thinking you were simply looking to buy a property?'

'But I am,' he assured her. 'It was you who introduced the subject telling me you wanted children. I feel the same way

I want a wife and family. It's predictable I suppose. I never really had one.'

'So what's wrong with advertising?' she suggested helpfully.

'Nothing whatsoever,' he said. 'We guys live in such isolation it's not easy to find partners.'

'I understand that,' she said, 'having been reared on the land. I have a feeling, though, if you do advertise you'll be inundated with answers.'

'I'm counting on it. In the meantime, there's *you*!' He flickered a silver glance at her.

It was pathetic, but thrills ran down her spine. 'It's like I told you, Rory Compton. Count me out!'

His handsome face was openly mocking. 'I know better than to argue.'

'That's a relief.' She felt a flush over her whole body.

Footsteps echoed in the hallway. In the next minute Chloe bustled in, eyes wide as she tried to gauge the atmosphere. From the look that came over her face she could have suspected amazing sex on the kitchen table. 'What in the world are you doing?' she asked, transferring her glance from one to the other.

'My fault,' Rory said, and flashed Allegra a smile.

Chloe's cheeks smarted. 'I just thought you might need some help?'

'We're fine thanks, Chloe,' Allegra said pleasantly. 'You can play Mother and wheel the trolley out if you like.'

Forty minutes later Rory was sitting in the passenger seat of the station Jeep with Chloe at the wheel. So far he could see work around Naroom had all but come to a stop. Why wouldn't it without an overseer to run it? Whatever had persuaded Mrs Sanders to sack her late husband's right hand man? It didn't make sense unless that was confirmation she had no intention of remaining on the land. Even then it was counter productive to allow the property to decline. He had seen around the homestead and liked it. It was spacious, comfortable, attractive. The outbuildings for the most part were in good condition. Now he asked Chloe to stop while he spoke to one of the stockmen who was driving a small mob of healthy looking beasts towards the creek.

'We'd be mighty pleased if a good man could buy the place,' the stockman confided within minutes of Rory's calling out to him. He was only too ready to talk and hopefully hold on to his job. 'Things have gone from bad to worse since the Boss died and Jack left. Jack Nelson was the overseer here for the past ten years with no complaints from the Boss, but Jack and the Missus couldn't see eye to eye. Or even half an eye come to that. She never wanted to spend any money maintaining the place. It was a real battle trying to get any money out of her for anything, even paying the vet. Jack reckoned she was only waiting for a buyer so she could sell up. The only one who loves the place is Miss Allegra. Miss Chloe now—I can see her back there in the Jeep—you want to strap yourself in—she won't do no rough work. Not much of a rider, either, which is pretty funny when to see Miss Allegra in the saddle does a man's heart good. She can handle most of the jobs on the station, too. Her dad taught her. Chloe, now, always liked to spend her time indoors with her mum. Both of them are bone lazy if you ask me. Hell, don't tell her that. I could lose my job.' He shut up abruptly.

Back in the Jeep Rory would have liked to suggest he take over the driving but didn't want to hurt Chloe's feelings. She didn't so much steer as wrestle with the wheel. One of her little foibles was hitting as many pot holes and partially submerged rocks as she could, sniffing them out like a heat-seeking missile. It was almost as if it were her bounden duty.

Then she groaned aloud as the vehicle reacted with a stomach churning kangarooing. Excuses ranged from, 'Whoops, didn't see that!' to 'That wasn't there last time!' Maintenance on the Jeep would run heavily to shock absorbers he reckoned.

'What did Gallagher have to say?' she asked when they resumed their seats after another bout of catapulting.

Rory thought it better not to pass on Gallagher's indiscretions. 'Nothing much. Just saying hello.'

'It's a wonder Mum didn't sack him along with Jack Nelson,' Chloe muttered, incredibly clipping a branch of a tree.

'Why's that?' Rory wondered how Chloe could possibly drive in a city or even a small town without hitting everything in her path. He even began to wonder if she'd had any proper driving lessons or simply got behind the wheel one day without bothering about lessons or a licence. He recalled he and Jay could drive around the station from a very early age.

'Cheeky bugger! Not respectful enough to Mum or me.' Chloe bridled.

'Who, Nelson or Gallagher?' Both that voice in his head said.

'Both,' Chloe confirmed, her pretty mouth tightening. 'It would be wonderful if you really liked the place, Rory. No one ever thought Dad would die so young. Mum and I are lost without him. Running a station needs a man. Dad needed a son. Instead he got Allegra and me,' she said wryly. 'I stayed. I was the loyal one. Allegra cleared off as soon as she could.'

'Oh, yes, when was this?' He tried not to sound too interested when he found himself avid for information.

'She insisted on going to university while I had to stay at home. Mum needed me. It's so lonely out here a girl could go ape. Afterwards Allegra landed a magazine job. We all know why. She's the perfect clothes horse and she *does* have good taste although it took a few years before she got the big promotion.'

'Was this before or after she married?' Rory asked, in-
igued Allegra might have kept working when she had
arried a rich man.

'The promotion?' She took such a lengthy look at him,
ory was forced to put a steadying hand on the wheel.

'Yes.'

Chloe placed her hand gently over his and took a while to
ke it off. 'She was fashion editor when she met Mark. She
ould easily have quit her job and devoted herself to being a
ood wife to Mark, but she didn't. I think a man deserves that,
on't you? He's *such* a lovely man, too, and she *dumped* him.
ask you! Dump the love of your life?'

'Obviously he wasn't,' Rory suggested, not trying all that
ard to dull the sarcasm.

'Seems not,' Chloe sighed and headed into a clump of
rambles. 'Mum and I really took to him. He's so handsome
nd clever *and* rich and he worshipped her. It's a bit weird isn't
 the way men worship beautiful women? I mean beauty's
nly a tiny fraction of what a real woman is all about. I tell
ou when she left him Mum and I were gobsmacked. We even
ought he might top himself.'

'Surely not!' Rory groaned before he could help himself.
Your father liked him, too?' He wanted some perspective on
e worshipping husband. Not that he exactly blamed him,
ny fraction or not.

Pretty Chloe scowled darkly. 'Oh, as far as Dad was con-
erned no one was good enough for Allegra!' she said, her
oice betraying her intense jealousy. 'You've no idea what it
as like for me when we were growing up. Allegra always
anting the attention and getting it from Dad. Allegra could
e an absolute *pig*!' She paused a moment to cool down. She
idn't want Rory getting the wrong idea about her. 'We're half
isters, you know.'

'Allegra did tell me,.' Rory admitted, surprised they were any relation at all.

'She would. No matter how much Mum and I tried she would never let us love her and Mum's the sweetest woman who ever drew breath.'

Rory fought a wry smile.

'I hesitate to say this,' Chloe continued with some relish, 'in fact it hurts me, but it might help you understand. My beautiful sister is pretty shallow. I don't think there's a man alive who could make her happy.' To reinforce her opinion Chloe hit the steering wheel with her open palm.

Sibling rivalry could be absolutely deadly Rory thought. Potentially so could Chloe's driving. 'That's your opinion, Chloe, is it? And what about you?' Rory kept his eyes glued ahead for more likely obstacles. If he'd only known what going for a drive with Chloe held in store! 'What are your plans if and when the station is sold?'

Chloe swung her head to beam at him. A woman just waiting to be hit by Cupid's arrow. 'I'm going to find myself a man,' she confessed with a dimpled grin. 'I'm going to have a Big White Wedding I'll always remember. And I won't have Allegra for my damned bridesmaid,' she tacked on wrathfully, heading towards a solitary gum tree like it was a designated pit stop. 'You can be sure of that!'.

Rory gently nudged the wheel. 'Obviously a sore point?' The reason wasn't lost on him.

'Well, I won't want her upstaging me on the best day of my life.' Inexplicably she braked hard as if they were coming to a set of traffic lights mysteriously erected in the bush. 'Can you blame me?' Satisfied about whatever it was—he didn't have a clue—she picked up speed again. 'I won't even let her meet my husband until after we're married just to be on the safe side. I won't be like her, either. Sadly she

uld only stay married five minutes. Marriage is forever,
ory, don't you think?'

He must have lost a layer of skin. Either that or it was the
ay Chloe was affecting him. 'Absolutely,' he said, 'or I'd
ant my money back.'

ney insisted he stay for a late lunch again prepared and
rved by Allegra who, as far as Rory could see, could get a
b at a top restaurant.

'Great meal, Allegra,' he complimented her. In fact it was
e best meal he'd had for quite a while, outside dinner with
e Cunninghams.

Chloe blushed fiercely. 'It's only a chicken dish,' she
binted out with a flick of the head, though she had not only
verloaded her plate she had scoffed the lot.

'The secret's in the spices,' Allegra told him, ignoring her
ster, instead of giving her the thump on the back of the head
e deserved. 'I'd be glad to give you the recipe to hand on.'

'Perfect,' he said.

'Hand on ? Who to?' Chloe looked baffled, staring from
e to the other in an effort to get them to divulge the secret.

'Rory is compiling a cookbook to hand over to his future
ife,' Allegra said.

'Good heavens! Are you really?' Chloe looked fascinated
/ such a thing. After all she had a glory box.

'I hadn't been thinking of it,' Rory confessed. 'Now I'm
onvinced I should do it.'

'Anyone special in your life, Rory?' Valerie asked, irri-
ted beyond measure by the constant exchanges between
eir visitor and Allegra and trying none too successfully not
show it.

He shook his head. 'No, not really, Mrs. Sanders.' He gave
er an easy smile.

'What's wrong with all the girls then?' Valerie favoure
him with a girlish one of her own. 'I would have thought you'
be fighting them off?'

Chloe, mouth slightly open, looked like she felt exactl
the same way.

'A man doesn't get to meet too many where I come from
Rory explained. 'The desert is about as remote as one can get

'Well then I'm sure you'll do better here,' Valerie sai
with great satisfaction, aiming a fond glance in her daugl
ter's direction.

Rory vowed there and then not to give Chloe the slighte
encouragement.

He took his leave of them thirty minutes later saying he'd hav
to think things over before getting back to them.

'Naturally' Valerie smiled and touched him gently on th
arm. 'We have to put our heads together, too.'

'Walk out to the car with me.' Rory managed to get off
quick aside to Allegra as Valerie wheeled about to have
word—never mind what it was—with her daughter.

'Very well.' Allegra led the way down the front steps, full
expecting Chloe to seize the moment and race after them. A
right, Chloe didn't normally race, but there was always th
first time. She had obviously taken a shine to Rory. Eve
Valerie had broken out into sunny smiles. One had to be
good looking young man to get one.

Strangely Chloe didn't come after them. There was onl
one explanation. It was too hot. 'So do you want to tell m
your thoughts now?' she asked as Rory fell in alongside he
She really liked the way she had to look up to him. In her hig
heels she and Mark had been fairly level.

'Your stepmother made a huge tactical error sacking you
overseer,' he commented in a crisp voice.

'Tell me something I don't know,' she sighed. 'Jack got on with everybody.' Except Valerie.

'Obviously he found it pretty hard going with your stepmother.'

Not wanting to criticise Valerie, Allegra said nothing.

'Surely you have a big stake in seeing the place is run properly?' Rory prompted, looking down at her flaming head. For some reason—again beyond him—he felt he could talk to her like he'd known her for ever. She was tall for a woman, around five-eight but to him she *felt* small. Indeed he'd had extreme difficulty keeping the *feel* of her out of his dreams. But there was no way he could volunteer that.

'That's why I'm here.' She showed a little flash of temper. 'Losing Dad was a great blow for all of us. Dad was the one who held us all together. With him gone I'm very much afraid I'll be minus what family I have left. Val and I never did get on.'

'Actually I can understand that,' he said laconically.

When Val had been on her best behaviour, Allegra thought. He should come on them unexpectedly. 'The thing is I was fatally blemished in my stepmother's eyes because I resemble my mother. Val suffered from the second wife syndrome. It's a very hurtful and wounding situation.'

Rory nodded. 'Skewed by the dagger of jealousy! Have you all come to some agreement on an asking price?'

'Not as yet,' she said.

'You *are* going to be able to work it out, right?' he asked dryly.

'Don't worry, we will. I take it you feel you can do something with the place?'

'Not feel, *know*,' he said, sounding utterly confident.

'Ah, the arrogance of achievement!' she said. 'Word is *you* ran your family station?'

'Jay and I.' He put her straight. 'I love my brother.'

'But he's not the cattleman in the family?'

'Would you believe he wanted to be a doctor?'

She picked up on the sadness, the regret. 'So, what stopped him? What finer calling could there be?'

'He's my father's heir, Allegra,' he pointed out. 'That says it all.'

'Okay. I understand. And I don't.' For total strangers they had moved quickly to a very real communication, no matter how edgy. 'It seems to me Jay should have fought for his dream, instead of letting it die a slow death.'

'Only life has a way of falling short of our dreams,' he said, ever sensitive to any criticism of his brother. 'So what decided you to scuttle *your* dream?' he questioned, combining a real desire to know with that little flash of sexual hostility.

'Scuttle is entirely the wrong word.' She gave him her own admonishing glance. 'I wanted to *cure* the situation. My dream was to find harmony and fulfilment. I thought I had a fighting chance with Mark but it blew up in my face like Krakatoa.'

'So you took the only course open to you. You bolted?' He was determined to know.

'What does anyone do when they find out they've made a big mistake,' she asked, very soberly. 'Now I've got to get my life back on track. Incidentally I'm stunned I'm talking like this to a near stranger.'

'It *is* a bit eerie,' he agreed. 'I'm not always like this with strange women, either. Then again we can think of it as pouring out a life story to the person sitting next to us on a plane.'

She laughed. 'I assure you I've never done it. There's too much to you, Rory Compton. Darkness, Lightness. Now I think back, I realise I was running away. I love Naroom. I love station life. After all it's what I was bred to. Yet I was impelled to change my life. It wasn't the best reason to marry.'

'You obviously weren't prepared to stick it out for the next forty years.'

It was said in a voice that so infuriated her, she wanted to
lap him. 'It strikes me that's none of your business.'

'True. It's just that I'm dying to know. How long was it
gain?'

'I repeat. None of your business, Compton,' she returned
oolly. 'You don't approve of what I did, do you?' She came
o a standstill staring up into his dynamic face.

He almost reached out to tuck a stray lock of her hair
ehind her ear. 'I don't approve of divorce in general, Allegra,
eing a child of divorce. Not unless there's a very good and
ressing reason. Which you may well have. Forgive me for
ot minding my own business.'

'You know what they say. Curiosity killed the cat.'

'Curiosity isn't the right word. It implies a passing interest.
aspire to seeing more of you, Miss Allegra. For better or
vorse, we seem to have bonded. I haven't as yet figured out
vhy. There's one thing jumps to mind. Your cooking. A
voman's ability to put out a good meal finds high favour with
nost men. Other things about you, however, could scare me.'

She acknowledged the mocking glitter in his eyes with a
ght smile. 'It's hard to believe any woman could scare you.
3y the way, it amazes me—I'm not a short woman—but just
ooking up at you makes me feel dizzy.'

Hell, he felt dizzy just looking down at her. 'Would you
elieve you appear *small* to me?'

'Then I'll definitely stick to high heels,' she said.

He had a sudden vision of her walking up the
'unningham's staircase, with him admiring her legs. 'When
ou get to know me you'll realise I am scarable,' he said with
grin. 'Is that a word?'

'They let in new words every day.' They walked on. 'I
now you worry about your brother. I know you're desper-
tely unhappy beneath the dark Byronic façade.'

'*Please.*' So self-assured, he looked embarrassed.

She decided being able to embarrass him pleased her 'Okay,' she scoffed. 'So there's too much romance about Byror for you. Do you know I actually cooked that special lunch for you today because you've lost weight even since we met.'

'Well fancy!' He gasped in mock surprise. 'You mean you've been studying me with those amazing blue eyes?'

'I figure if *you* can look, so can I,' she answered crisply. 'Why did you want me to walk with you? Any particular reason?'

'I'm certain you walk a lot faster than Chloe,' was hi flippant response. 'Why? Did you have something better to do? Like spend more time with your stepmother and sister?

'Your family's not everything it should be.' She struck back

'Indeed it's not,' he agreed with a rasp in his voice. 'Wher you think about it, Allegra, the two of us have lived through a lot of stuff. Though I've never had the unfortunate experi ence of being burned by a bad marriage.'

'What about singed by a love affair that went wrong?' she asked with feigned sweetness.

He only smiled. 'Not yet.'

'Don't lay money on it not happening,' she said. 'Falling in love is a dangerous business.'

'And your love for your ex-husband wasn't unconditional?'

'You're making me angry, Rory,' she said. In fact he wa making her heart pound.

'And I don't blame you. I apologise. You raise my bloo pressure, too.'

They had reached his Toyota, now Rory opened the driver's door.

'Don't count on getting this place cheap, either,' she warned, conscious her body was throbbing in the oddest way

'Then I'll blame you for pushing up the price.' He turne to fully face her.

They were so close, on a panicked reflex, Allegra stepped
ck, her heart almost leaping into her throat. It was her turn
r embarrassment to wash over her.

'So long, Allegra,' he said, his eyes holding a wealth of
ockery. He sketched a brief salute. 'I'll get back to you in
lay or two.'

'You've made up your mind now,' She slammed his door
ut, beating him to it.

He studied her through the open window. The sun was
ning her glowing head to fire. 'Be sure of it,' he said.

CHAPTER FOUR

JAY paused for a minute to catch his breath. His arms we▸
aching from thrashing through the lignum swamp. His khal
bush shirt was soaked with sweat, his jeans soaked with
green slime and swamp water up to the knees. He and a coupl
of the men had been hunting up a massive wild boar as big ▸
a calf that kept threatening the herd. They had chased it int
the deepest reaches of the swamp where a man on his ow
would find it very easy to get lost. The swamp was home ▸
countless water birds and pelicans, but was spell-bound to tł
aborigines who shivering in fear, refused to go into it. Ja
didn't altogether blame them. An unearthly yellow glo
emanated from the place, seeping into the air. Rory, of cours
afraid of nothing always said it was a sulphur sprin₃
Whatever the eerie glow was, it was almost impossible to g▸
into the swamp's deepest recesses without a machete. A goc
enough reason for the boar to make its home in the den₃
thickets, out of the path of danger where it could wallow ▸
its heart's content in the mud.

It had made one last stand, its ugly head lowered for a fin₃
charge. It glared at them with its little reddened eyes, a ferc
cious looking animal, its coarse black bristles caked in mu
and slime. Two powerful yellowish tusks protruded from i▸

wer jaw, curving upwards in half circles. Sharp tusks that
uld easily disembowel a man or gore him to death. Spear
rrying aborigines on the plain, would have charged the beast
d killed it, a manoeuvre so dangerous it made Jay shudder
st to think of it, though he knew boar hunting had been con-
dered an exciting sport for hundreds of years. Jay got off a
ngle clean shot to the boar's heart. Its bulk quivered for a
oment on its short powerful legs, then it rolled over with a
ud squelching sound into the foul smelling mud.

hat exploit had taken them far afield and it was a long ride
ck before Jay reached the home compound.

  He had truly believed he fully appreciated just how much
rd yakka Rory put in, day in and day out—how much re-
onsibility he assumed without saying a word. Rory had a
tural affinity with animals; all sorts of animals from the
ldest rogue brumby hell-bent on freedom to the most docile
lf. Rory wouldn't have spent the best part of the afternoon
cking down that boar. He could read the signs as clearly as
y aboriginal. Rory had only been gone a month and already
 was sorely missed by all.

  Jay missed him terribly. First as a brother and his best friend:
en as a buffer between him and their father and thirdly as the
ttleman, the Boss-man, who ran Turrawin. Rory was the
mpton every last station employee deferred to and took
ders from without complaint. Rory was a natural born leader.
ch men didn't come along every day. Their father, Bernard,
y had long since recognised, had little going for him these
ys but bluster and a whiplash tongue. With Rory gone there
as animosity where there had never been before. Not only
at, it was on the rise among the station staff. Not towards *him*
rsonally—he got on well enough with everyone—but the
ole situation. Not content with ordering Rory off the station,

their father had let it be known Rory wasn't coming bac[k]
Further more Rory had been disinherited.

What that had achieved was nigh on catastrophic. It ha[d]
bonded everyone against his father. While the men had great[ly]
admired and respected Rory, working happily in the sadd[le]
for him from dawn to dusk, they were becoming discontente[d]
and occasionally rebellious under him. Okay they liked him—
they even felt sorry for him having the father he did—but the[y]
didn't look to him as the boss.

He wasn't a cattleman, though God knows he'd struggle[d]
to become one. The trouble was his heart wasn't in it and [he]
wasn't half tough enough. He wasn't much good at givi[ng]
orders, either, or even knowing what best to do in difficu[lt]
situations when Rory, the man of action, had always come [up]
with a solution right off the top of his head. Jay's only gi[ft]
was fixing things, especially machinery. Rory had constant[ly]
reassured him that was a considerable gift. He could take a[ny]
piece of faulty station machinery apart and put it togeth[er]
again in fine working order. Just like he had once longed [to]
put the damaged human body back together.

He was thirty years of age, two years Rory's senior, but [he]
still longed for the beautiful woman who had been his moth[er.]
She had understood him but she had never been strong enoug[h]
to withstand their father. She was scared of him the same w[ay]
Jay had been scared of him. The only one who wasn't scar[ed]
was Rory. But even Rory had been known to flinch aw[ay]
from their father's vicious tongue.

Now that Rory was gone their father took it out on him.

He returned to the homestead at dusk, cursing the fact, as [he]
did every day, his father was such a severe man who the[se]
days possessed not even a chink of lightness of soul. Berna[rd]
Compton had become damned impossible. When Jay entere[d]

he kitchen through the back door prior to taking a shower in he adjacent mudroom, he found his father slouched over the uge pine table, a whiskey bottle near his hand. Jay never remembered his father drinking so much but these past weeks e'd been getting into it as if alcohol took his mind off his roubles and what was already going wrong on the station. It vas his grandfather and the Compton men before him to vhom they owed the success of Turrawin. Then Rory. The ecessary skills and attributes had skipped a generation.)ddly enough, his father, like him, was excellent with machinery but he took little pride in Jay's inherited ability. In fact e went out of his way to deride it.

'That's all you're bloody good for, son. Tinkering about!'

His tinkering had saved the station a lot of money.

3ernard Compton looked up as Jay entered the room. There vas no welcoming smile on his heavy handsome face but a cowl. His once brilliant dark eyes were badly bloodshot. There's a couple of postcards from your brother,' he said, aking a gulp of his drink.

'You've read them?' Jay moved towards the table, feeling rush of pleasure and relief at hearing from Rory again.

'Why not? They're bloody postcards aren't they?'

'They're addressed to me,' Jay pointed out quietly, picking hem up. 'You shouldn't have sent Rory away, Dad. We can't o without him.'

'I'm not asking him to come back, if that's what you think.' 3ernard Compton's face was set grimly. 'I don't get down on ny knees to anyone least of all my own son. No respect, ory. No respect at all. Looking at me with his mother's eyes.'

'Mum's beautiful eyes,' Jay said, his glance devouring vhat was written on the two postcards, each from different)utback towns. 'He's at a place called Jimboorie. Or he was.'

'I can read,' Bernard said roughly, staring up at his son. Jay was a handsome big fellow, strong and clever, but for God knows what reason glaringly inadequate when it came to running the station. 'So what do you want me to do about it?'

'Beg Rory to come home, Dad,' Jay answered promptly. 'The men look to Rory, not me.' *Not to you, either,* hung heavily in the air.

'He made his bed now he's got to lie in it,' Bernard Compton said. 'What we need is an overseer given you're so hopeless.'

'You're not much better,' Jay retorted, almost beyond caring what his father thought. 'Why didn't I have the guts to do what I always wanted to do?'

'Become a doctor?' Bernard snorted, and threw back the whiskey.

'I'd have been a good doctor,' Jay said in his quiet way. 'It' in my genes. I should have pushed for it.'

His father hooted. 'You've never pushed for anything in your life.'

Not with a father I hated and feared. 'Maybe there's still time to make plans,' Jay said. 'Rory told me there was.'

'That's because *he* wants Turrawin.' His father told him with a savage laugh. 'There's no end to your gullibility, son. Rory wants Turrawin,' Bernard repeated.

'Well, I don't want it, Dad,' Jay replied, his unhappiness growing more unbearable every day.

'Why, you gutless wonder! I'm ashamed of you, Jay,' Bernard Compton thundered, striking the table with his large fist.

'Do you think I don't know that?' Jay asked in a weary voice. 'You've bludgeoned me over the head with it for years, Dad. But my inadequacies are modest compared to yours. All you're good for is letting loose with the venom.'

'Why you—!' Bernard Compton, his face flushed a dark red, started to rise, but Jay, a powerful young man, shoved him back down on his chair. 'When I was a kid I used to find you very frightening. Mum did, too. But no more. I pity you from the bottom of my heart. You're a hollow man. Rory should have Turrawin. I'm the one who has to give up on this life I was never meant to lead.'

'What are you saying?' Bernard Compton's bloodshot eyes were filled with shock and disbelief.

'You heard me. Rory should have Turrawin otherwise his historic station will go steadily downhill. Only Rory can save it.'

'Over my dead body,' Bernard Compton exploded, glaring at his son.

'Why do you hate him so much?' Jay marvelled. 'He's your son, isn't he? Is there some bloody thing we don't know? Is that why Mum left? What's the goddamn mystery?'

Bernard Compton gave an awful grunt, clutching the whiskey bottle and pouring himself another double shot. 'Of course Rory is my son, you idiot. And I don't hate him. I bloody well admire him like I admired my old man. But there was to be a lot of space between us. I don't want him on my territory.'

'You're afraid of him aren't you? He's everything you wanted to be. Grandad loved him so much. He loved *me*, but always knew Rory was the favourite.'

'That old bastard!' Bernard swore blearily. 'He certainly didn't love me. He always made me feel a fool.'

'Then I'm sorry, but it was never his intention. Grandad was really good man. I'll stay with you, Dad, until we get a competent overseer in place. I thought we could bring Ted Warren in from Mariji. He's more competent than I am to handle things. Then I'm going to get a new life. Up until now I've always had the weird feeling I'm on hold with nothing to hope for. That has to change. But first, I'm going to find my brother.'

* * *

Allegra stood on the front verandah watching life giving rain pour down over the burdened eaves in silver curtains so heavy it was impossible to see out into the home gardens. It was well over a week now since Rory Compton had made the two-hour journey from Jimboorie township to Narooma with his offer: an offer Valerie and Chloe had near jumped at. She on the other hand had made it abundantly clear it wasn't enough, although she pretty well believed him when he said it was the best he could do. He didn't seem the man to try to beat them down. Clay Cunningham didn't think so, either. She'd already had a conversation with Clay, a man she trusted, who had revealed a little more about Rory Compton's situation. It was true his brother, Jay was to inherit historic Turrawin. True by all accounts—word in the far flung Outback flew around with astonishing speed—Bernard Compton had disinherited his younger son.

Rory Compton was no longer part of a wealthy family of pioneering cattle barons. Times for Rory had changed. He was out on his own albeit with the wherewithal to purchase a smallish run. Nothing that could possibly match what he had come from, but a property a man with his talents could build on and make prosper. Allegra was sure of it.

Rory Compton was a man of substance at twenty-eight. No great age. Her father would have judged him square in the mould of builder-expander. A man who exuded all the drive, ambition, know-how and ideas to turn middle of the road Naroom into a financial success. After that, she supposed, he would move on to bigger and better things. His offer had been basically, their reserve $3.5 million. She was sticking out for $4 million knowing despite depreciation and a big drop in stock numbers, Naroom was worth that. Or were her emotions too heavily involved? Naroom was her *home*.

The magic of the place! Yet she seemed to be the only one

ow her dad was gone to feel it. Anyway as far as borrowing went
ory Compton still had his name. A name to be reckoned with.
is bank had approved his loan in what seemed to her record
me. Her gut feeling was the bank could go $500,000 more.

No surprises a huge family fight had developed. Her on one
de: Valerie and Chloe on the other. If she had ever thought
d hoped there was some love between her and her half-sister
e soon found out when the chips were down, there wasn't.
ven thinking about the things Valerie and Chloe had said to
r brought the sting of tears to her eyes. At one point she even
ought Valerie would come at her in a rush of physical rage.
alerie was not to be thwarted. She wanted out like a wild horse
anted its freedom. And don't for the love of God get in the
ay. Whatever Valerie wanted, so did Chloe. The gang of two.

It wasn't as though she had been adamant with a no. Their
mbined clout equalled hers. All she wanted was a better
fer. Or the opportunity at least to see if he could come up with
better offer? Surely that was reasonable? She was doing this
r her dad, not for herself. His memory. Yet Valerie and Chloe
d branded her with every unjust name they could think of.

'I'll tell you straight! I despise you for being so selfish!'
alerie had raged. 'Why did you come back here? We
dn't want you.'

It doesn't take a lot of words to tear a heart out. What point
saying she had a perfect right to come back. Naroom was
much her home as theirs. More. But they obviously thought
r marriage, however short, and their long tenancy down-
aded her rights.

The following morning they left in a great flurry, catching
charter flight to Brisbane.

'I'm going to make it my business to consult with a top
wyer regarding *my* rights,' Valerie announced a half an hour
fore their departure. 'I was Llew's wife! Surely to God I had

the stronger claim? But no, I finished up with a mere quarte
of everything.'

'A quarter of the estate amounts to quite a lot, Val.' Allegr
tried to get a word in edgeways.

But Valerie wasn't prepared to listen. 'I'm going to se
about contesting the will. It's an outrage your share was doubl
mine. Anyone would side with me on that one. The *wife* shoul
be the main beneficiary. I know you worked on your fathe
You kept at him and at him until he saw things your way.'

A wave of futility crested then crashed on Allegra. For he
and Valerie to reconcile was unimaginable. 'That is patentl
untrue, Valerie. For your information Dad and I never ever dis
cussed his will.'

'And who would believe you?' Valerie countered, her eye
flashing anger and disbelief. 'Anyway I can't stand aroun
arguing with you. We have a plane to catch.'

'Good but before you go I want you to know I have no in
tention of holding up a sale if that's what you want. All I'r
seeking is the best possible price we can get.'

'Just see you stick to that!' Valerie responded, her voic
charged with venom.

There was, alas, little hope what was left of family coul
survive. Her father gone Allegra felt she was well and trul
on her own.

By late morning the rain had ceased and the sun came out i
all its glory, dispersing the clouds. Allegra took the opportu
nity of saddling up Cezar, her father's big handsome bay, an
riding out to check on the herd. After one torrential downpou
the creek that had been low for so long had risen a goo
metre, the surging brown water frothed with white. It course
between its green banks, spewing up spray wherever it en
countered boulders and rocks. She had already given th

der to move the stock in case there were further downpours, hich was a strong possibility. It was the monsoon season in e tropical North. Anything was possible; deep troughs, clones. The cattle were now grazing all over the flats on ther side of the creek. They all knew what flash floods were ke. They had all seen dead bloated cattle with terror carved to their faces. It was not a sight one forgot.

When she was satisfied everything was moving according plan she rode back to the homestead, rejoicing in a world the in had washed clean. She loved the air after the rain. She loved ling beneath the trees getting showered with water from the ipping branches. Everything about her, body and spirit, joiced in the great outdoors. For sure she had made a name r herself working as a fashion editor. She knew she was very od at her job. She had natural flair but she had always known here her heart was. It was the *land* that made her happy.

She was approaching the house when she saw with a flare excitement as big as a bonfire: Rory Compton's Land ruiser parked in the driveway. A moment later she saw his ll rangy figure walk down the front steps, making for his hicle. Finding no one at home he was obviously leaving. at couldn't be allowed to happen. This man was too much her mind.

Allegra urged the bay into a gallop.

e saw her coming. The bay she was riding was too big and ost likely too strong for most women but she was handling beautifully. She was wearing a cream slouch hat crammed wn on her head, but her dark red hair was streaming neath it like a pennant in the wind. He remembered what beautiful natural rider his mother had been. How he had ved to watch her. He was painfully aware his love for the

woman who had borne him wasn't buried so deep it couldn[
resurface at some time. A tribute to motherhood he suppose[

He found he loved watching this woman, too. Allegr[
Hamilton was luring him like a moth drawn compulsively [
a lamp. From out of nowhere she was all over his life. He wa
even starting to miss her when he didn't see her. He was eve
starting to imagine her there beside him. Hell, he wante[
more of her. More of her company. The good Lord had eithe
answered his prayers or sent him one heck of a problem.

She reined in a foot or two away from him, one han
tipping her hat the brim turned up on both sides, further bac
on her head. Her posture was proud and elegant. God, what
the matter with me? he thought

The answer came right away. You've fallen fathoms dee
in love.

'What brings you here, Rory Compton?' Her eye
sparkled all over him, his face and his body, setting up
chain of spine tingles.

He damn nearly said, *you*. But no way could her feeling
be as well developed as his. He made do with business. 'I'v
come with my final offer,' he explained.

'Ah, so you've got one?' She dismounted in one swif
graceful movement, swinging her long slender leg up an
over the horse's back.

'That's some animal,' he said, running his eyes over th
handsome beast.

'Cezar.' She patted the bay's neck affectionately. 'Ceza
was my father's horse.'

'I should have known. He's too big and too powerful to b
a woman's horse.'

'Are you saying I can't handle him?' She had to narrow he
eyes against the glare.

He spread his hands. 'Never, my lady. It was a pleasure t

watch you. You're a fine horsewoman. My mother was, too.' He hadn't intended to mention his mother at all. It just happened.

Her beautiful face softened into tenderness. 'You miss her terribly, don't you?'

'Here, let me do that,' he said, ignoring her question because he was too moved by it, coming forward so he could remove the saddle from her heated horse.

'It's okay,' she said, turning her head. 'Here comes Wally. He'll take care of it.'

'Fine.' Rory watched as a wiry-looking lad of around sixteen—he vaguely recognised him—jogged towards them, coming from the direction of the stables. He had a big cheerful grin all over his face. 'Thought I saw you comin' back, Miss Allegra.'

'We both wanted that ride, Wally,' she said and handed him the reins. 'Look after him for me, would you? You remember Mr Compton?'

'Sure do!' The boy, part aboriginal, studied Rory with obvious liking. 'Gunna buy the place, boss?'

'Allow us to work that out, Wally, if you don't mind.' Allegra broke in, her tone mild.

'Sure, Miss Allegra.' Wally's grin stayed in place. He hadn't taken the slightest offence. He took the reins to lead Cezar away. 'Nice to see yah, Mr Compton.'

'So long, Wally.' Rory nodded casually. 'Be good now.'

'Come into the house,' Allegra said as she turned to Rory, truck by the dramatic foil his light eyes, tanned skin and black hair presented. He was so handsome it seemed to her he radiated a spell. She just hoped she was keeping her powerful response underwraps. But surely no red-blooded woman could fail to be aroused by such stunning masculinity, or not enjoy his male beauty. Even after the traumas of her broken marriage she couldn't help but wonder what he would be like in bed.

Face it. She'd been spending too much time wondering. At a time when she should be standing back, taking stock of her life, a new relationship had been thrown open. What to do with it? Briskly she made towards the front steps.

'So where are Valerie and Chloe?' Rory asked, as they moved into the empty house. He would have a huge job in front of him keeping up the businesslike aura.

'They won't be back here until next week,' Allegra said, throwing her cream hat unerringly onto a peg.

He saluted her aim with a clap. 'Are they taking a short holiday?' he asked. He wouldn't cry buckets if they weren't coming back.

'You could say that.' She turned to face him, filled with something very like joy. Where was all this leading? She only knew it was going too fast.

'Would it be considered impolite to ask why?' Rory stared back at her, drinking her in. She was wearing a mulberry coloured polo shirt over cream jodhpurs that showed off the slender length of her legs and her very neat butt. She didn't appear to be wearing any makeup at all. Just a touch of lipstick probably to protect her mouth, but her beauty was undiminished.

'You're loads better off not knowing!' Her answer was wry.

'Tell me. One would have to be massively insensitive not to pick up on the fact you women don't have a warm relationship.'

'Okay, we had an argument,' she confessed.

'I would never have guessed! It involved my offer and your decision not to accept it, of course.'

'Clairvoyant as well.' She turned to walk into the living room and he followed.

God, she could lead me anywhere, Rory thought, not altogether proud of the way he had fallen so easily for her. Did he actually *need* a mad passion? Surely he had decided he didn't. Yet he was thrilled and apprehensive at the same time

Their being alone together could only draw them closer. He already knew he was going to go along with it, even though he recognised she had the capacity to hurt him badly. This was a woman who would want to go back to her glamour job in the city. That was something to be feared.

You fool, Rory! This is getting altogether too serious.

He was getting right into the habit of communing with himself. Now he glanced around the comfortable living room. 'Family arguments are no fun.' Boy, didn't he have some experience!

'You can say that again,' she sighed. 'My family doesn't want me here anymore. That's it in a nutshell.'

'Okay let's sit down,' he said gently, seeing how much that hurt her.

'We're going to haggle?' She settled into an armchair indicating he take the one opposite.

'If you like. A cup of coffee would make me feel better.'

She sprang up as if remiss at not offering him one. 'Me, too!' She was becoming addicted to this man and in such a short while. Yet right from the beginning an intimacy had existed she had never shared with anyone else. Explain *that*? Come through to the kitchen,' she invited. 'We can haggle in there.'

It was a big kitchen but his presence filled it up. Allegra busied herself hunting out the coffee grinder then taking the beans from the refrigerator.

'I'll do that,' he offered, moving closer.

'Fine.' Even her pulses were doing an Irish reel. 'Count to twenty, that should do it.' She opened a cupboard and took out coffee cups and saucers, trying to tone herself down.

'The rain was wonderful,' he said when he finished grinding the beans and the kitchen was quiet again. 'I found myself standing out in it.'

'I can understand that.' She smiled. 'I did, too. I was pur posely riding under the trees so I could get a shower from th wet branches. Do you think we'll get more? Rain is so ver unpredictable.'

'Certain to,' he said.

'How do you know? Don't tell me it's your aching bones?'

'I can *feel* it. I can *smell* it,' he said. 'Besides the rain i coming down in bucket loads in the North. The last report heard a cyclone was forming in the Coral Sea. That's all it wil take. It's either flood or drought. If the cyclone develops an we get torrential rain, the Big Three—that's the Diamantina the Georgina and the Cooper—will bring the floodwater right down into our remote South-West corner. The Channe Country is one vast natural irrigation system as I'm sure yo know. You've never been there?'

'I regret to say, no. I spent years at boarding school, the university, then I married. But I will get there one day.'

'It would be nice to take you,' he said. 'The whole regio can flood without a drop of actual rain. Seen from the air i looks like the whole country is underwater.'

'Of course!' She looked across at him in quick realisa tion. 'You *would* see it from the air. You have your ow plane on Turrawin?'

He nodded. 'A Beech Baron and a couple of Bell helicop ters. We use the choppers a lot for mustering. We also use th services of an aerial mustering company from time to time Choppers have revolutionised the whole business.'

'I can imagine, with those vast areas.' She stopped what sh was doing to study him. 'But it can be dangerous? I've hear of many instances of fatal light aircraft and chopper crashes

'Very dangerous.' He shrugged the danger off. 'But it's ou way of life, Allegra. We have to keep our fears under control

'That's pretty amazing,' she said dryly.

'When fatalities happen our vast community shares in the
artbreak. We're all in it together. I've been in ground
arches and aerial searches in my time. We've had two major
cidents in the last twelve years on Turrawin. One death I
gret to say. A really good bloke, one of our regulars who
uld fly anything and land anywhere so no one worried about
n for quite a while. The other was a crash landing, but mer-
ully the pilot walked away. I've had a close call myself.
ace I came down in the middle of a big paperbark swamp.
the Territory I could have been taken by a croc, but we don't
ve any crocs in the desert. Well not anymore.' He smiled.
hough you can see them in our aboriginal rock paintings.'

She stared back at him fascinated. 'You have cave paint-
gs on Turrawin?'

'We don't advertise, but yes. Some of them are amazing.
ae cave in particular is guaranteed to make you believe in
e Spirit Guardians. The hairs stand up on my forearms and
onsider myself pretty cool.'

'You *are* cool.' She laughed. 'I'd love to see that cave myself.'

'I wish I could take you there.'

'That would be wonderful,' she admitted recklessly. 'We
n't have anything like that around here.'

'I know.'

His mouth, quirked as it was now, was framed by the
kiest little brackets. She realised she watched for those
oments. That was what falling in love was all about. It
emed that for her this was the classic coup de foudre. Which
no means guaranteed things were going to turn out fine she
minded herself. As for it happening at such a turning point
her life she was beyond thought.

'You're very passionate about your desert domain, aren't
u?' She said, knowing he would be passionate about
ost things.

'Yes, ma'am.' His crystalline eyes looked right into hers. 'I
like no other place on earth and Jay and I have managed to s
quite a few. Australia is the oldest continent on earth. I think th
accounts for a lot of the extraordinary mystique. It's the tim
lessness, the antiquity, the aboriginal feel, the power of t
Dreamtime spirits. Then there's the colour of the place…t
vivid contrast between the fiery red earth and the cloudle
blue sky. Every country offers its great and its quiet wonder

'I've stayed a few times with friends, another cattle fami
who own and run a magnificent ranch in Colorado. They ha
the Rocky Mountains for a backdrop. It's like *wow*! Then v
had a great trip to Argentina a couple of years back. Busine
and pleasure. A wonderfully colourful and exciting place. V
loved it. We managed to get in a few games of polo while v
were there. They're the greatest as I'm sure you know. V
even got to fly over the Andes. I love flight. I love flyir
Being up there in the wild blue yonder all on your lonesor
It's tremendous!'

'Then you're going to miss it, aren't you?' she said, gettir
a clear picture of him seated at the controls of a plar
'Naroom doesn't run to light aircraft.'

He shrugged. 'Well you *are* much closer to civilisatic
Turrawin on the other hand is right on the edge of t
Simpson. The sand dunes there peak at around one hundr
feet and they run for a couple of hundred kilometres unbrok
the longest parallel sand dunes in the world. It's really ee
the way they bring to mind the inland sea of prehistory. I'
stood on top of our most famous dune, Nappanerica—'

'The Big Red?' She smiled, glad she knew the answer.

'The very same. A Simpson traveller, Dennis Bart
named it. It's closer to one hundred fifty feet. The mc
amazing little wildflowers come out after a shower. Not t
gigantic displays we get after flooding. But it's fascinating

dy the little fellas up close. There are so many you can't
ove without crushing them underfoot, but then they release
e most wonderful perfume. You think you've died and gone
Heaven.' He purposely didn't say he thought the fragrance
in to the fresh fragrance that came off her body.

'And after flooding?' she asked. 'I've seen marvellous pho-
graphic shots in calendars.'

'Allegra,' he said dryly, 'You have to see the real thing.' As
spoke he was imagining her with a diadem of yellow daisies
ound her head. As young boys he and Jay had fashioned them
: their mother. 'After heavy rain, the desert flora has no equal,'
said with unmistakably nostalgia. 'The landscape is com-
:tely carpeted by pink, white and yellow paper daisies. It's
e some great inland tide. They even sweep up to the stony
l country. Even the hills come alive with thousands of fluffy
ılla mulla banners and waving lambs tails. So many varieties
desert peas come out, fuchsias and hibiscus, our exquisite
sert rose. Nature's glory confronts you wherever you look.'

'It sounds wonderful,' she said, moved by the controlled
otion in his voice and face. Nostalgia was written all over
n 'The central plains must seem pretty tame to you after
ur desert home?'

He raised both his wide shoulders in a shrug, but he
ın't answer.

'Is there no hope of a reconciliation between you and your
her?' she dared to ask the question.

His face angled away from her, looked grim. 'I need to get
far away from my father as is humanly possible.'

Good God as bad as that!' she said, pondering the no-
lds-barred bitterness and hatreds in family life. 'It seems
me you're a son to be proud of.'

He looked up then to smile at her, the smile that was im-
ssible to resist. 'Why thank you, Miss Allegra.'

'I'm not trying to butter you up,' she said, a shade tartl
counteract that sexual radiance. 'Just a simple statemen
fact.' Belatedly she put the coffee on to perk. He was jus
interesting to talk to she had forgotten all about it. 'Take a s

He pulled out a chair, resting his strong tanned arms on
table. He was wearing a red T-shirt with his jeans, the fal
clinging to his wide shoulders and the taut muscular lin
his torso. It was hard to look past his physical magnetism
fact it was making her jumpy. So jumpy she felt if he touc
her she would fall to pieces. Wisely she stayed on the oppo
side of the table.

'So what have you got to tell me?'

He was as aware as she was of the glittering sexual tens
that stretched between them, but he tried to play it cool as
fitting a serious man. 'I can go a little higher with my bid

She raised an arched brow. 'How high is *a little*?'

He turned up his hands. 'We'll split it between $3.5 a
$4 million. My final offer, Mrs Hamilton, is $3.75.'

'That *Mrs* Hamilton might cost you,' she said frostily.

'What did he do to you?' The intense desire to reach
her—the desire he was endeavouring to keep on simmer
damned nearly boiled over.

'What's made you change your mind about me?' s
asked. 'When we first met it was like— What did she do
her poor husband?'

'I've had an epiphany,' he said, deciding there was saf
in being flippant. 'For one thing, you're a great cook.'

'So the fact I can cook swung it?' The coffee was perk
away merrily. She turned away to shift it off the heat.

'I'm joking!' There was amusement in his eyes.

'I know you are, Rory Compton,' she said tartly, betrayi
her stretched feelings. There was only one answer to all th
The question was when?

am trying to slow myself down. I don't want to frighten you away, but you're the most romantic, the most glamorous woman I've ever met. And you smell like a million crushed wildflowers.'

Her heart faltered, plunged on. 'That's one sweet compliment for a cautious man, Rory Compton.'

'I just can't help myself. There's something so right about you, Allegra. Too much danger, too.'

'In what way?'

He looked past her. 'I'm an Outback cattleman. You're a woman with a glamorous career in Sydney.'

'So I am,' she said, suddenly plummeted into bleakness.

He wanted to pull her into his arms, stroke that melancholy expression away, instead he spoke bracingly, trying to keep both of them on an even keel. 'It was one hell of a trip around the property with Chloe. Her driving isn't so much dangerous as unlawful. What about the two of us riding out? I know you've still got some good horses.'

Instantly she felt a surge of pleasure that blew her troubles away. 'Great minds think alike! I was planning that myself. You can ride Cezar if you like?' She was aware of her desire to see him on horseback. She hadn't the slightest doubt he'd been a superlative rider.

His eyes widened for a second. 'I'd really appreciate that, Allegra,' he said. 'And I'm honoured. Cezar is a splendid animal.'

'You're welcome.'

'Great!' He stood up, cattleman coming to the fore. 'I hope you've had your men shift the cattle off the river flats. If there is more rain the water will rise above the escarpments of the creek. It will run a bumper and then, you'll have trouble on your hands.'

Allegra rolled her eyes heavenwards. 'Do you think I don't know? I'm not stupid, Rory Compton.'

'I'm starting to think you're a paragon,' he said dryly.

Allegra took the final gulp of her coffee.

'Right!' He pushed back his chair. 'Let's get going while the sun's out.'

CHAPTER FIVE

HE WAS already acting like Naroom was his own, Allegra thought, torn between acceptance and an understandable sense of loss. It was midafternoon, stiflingly hot and humid even though the sun had disappeared under a great pile-up of incandescent clouds. The smell of sulphur was in the air. It was as though one only had to strike a match for the whole world to go up in flames. Even the birds had stopped singing, lapsing into the silence that precedes a storm. Presently a wind sprang up, gaining velocity. Spiralling whirlwinds danced across the darkening landscape sending out their own clouds of dust, leaves and split, sun-scorched grasses.

There was a lot of water stored in those ominous clouds. The rain couldn't have been more welcome but she dreaded the thought of hail. Many times in her life she'd seen it come down on Naroom with hellish fury, hailstones as big as cricket balls, bombarding the herd and sometimes killing the small game scurrying through the pastures.

Allegra roused herself from her thoughts. Rory hadn't been at all happy with the distance north of the homestead Gallagher and his off-sider Mick Evans had moved the cattle so he rode off with steely purpose to let them know. Allegra sat silently on her horse watching. There was always work to be done on a station; always another job.

Rory would get the men moving, she thought with satisfaction. It seemed only a man, a tough cattleman with a superior knowledge and experience of cattle could fill the shoes of Boss Man. Women need not apply. The outer areas of the run would be safe but he wanted *all* the cattle concentrated in the home pastures mustered and moved off the creek flats. One of the major problems with the station hands since her father's death, then the loss of their competent overseer—Valerie's disastrous decision—was that the men were sinking deeper and deeper into lethargy, understandably uncertain of their future when times weren't easy. Even the cook had taken off, but cooks were always guaranteed of a job.

Well, I gave them their orders, Allegra consoled herself. The *right* orders. 'Remember now. High out of the creek's reach!' It was clear they had only half done the job. She had fully intended to check on them. She knew she had to, but Rory's arrival had set her back. She watched him ride back to her, the stirring sight bringing the sting of tears to her eyes. Cezar was more than a touch temperamental but Rory wasn't having the slightest trouble making a near instant communication with her father's horse, essentially a one man horse although Cezar had gradually accepted her.

'You're not happy are you?' she asked, studying his expression as he reined in alongside.

'No, but there's no use worrying about it. We have to get cracking. We need to shift all the cows and calves on the other side across the creek.' There was a dark frown on his face. 'I've told those two layabouts if they're interested in holding on to a job they'd better shake themselves up. Big time. We'll never get the stock across if the creek starts flowing any faster. As it is we'll have to push them with stock whips. They're certain to be nervous, especially with this wind blowing up.' He glanced heavenward at the threatening sky. 'I've ser

allagher to get the Jeep and bring it down here. Some of
ose calves are pretty small. They'll hold the rest up. We can
ck 'em up and shove them in the back of the Jeep.'

'Right, boss!' She spoke in a voice of exaggerated respect.

'It needs to be done.' He gave her a querying look.

'Of course it does. Just having a little joke. I did tell
em, you know.'

'Obviously they weren't paying the right amount of atten-
n,' he said crisply. 'They will now. If you ride back to the
bles you can tell young Wally we need a hand. On the
uble. Doesn't anyone use their own initiative? What about
u?' He cast a dubious eye over her slender, ultrafeminine
me. 'I'll understand if you don't want to join in. It'll be hard
rk and we're pushed for time thanks to those two. We need
em otherwise you should sack them on the spot.'

'They need sacking,' she agreed. 'And don't be ridiculous.
f course I'll help. That's what I'm here for.' She wheeled her
rse's head about. 'They're all docile beasts on Naroom. We
n't have your mighty herds to contend with. No rogues, no
ld ones, no clean skins, either.'

'Off you go then,' he urged. 'We've got a lot to do before
e weather worsens.'

big storm broke around dusk but by then they had every last
wing beast up on high ground. Allegra's ears were ringing
m the crack of the whips. They kept them sailing well
ove the backs of the herd while the loud sound drove them
. Darkness was closing in fast, the sun almost swallowed
. The familiar landscape was shrouded in a sodden mist that
enched them in seconds.

'Dig your heels in!' he called to her.

She didn't need to be told twice. The temperature had
opped considerably and she was shivering. When they arrived

back at the homestead, the two of them ran quickly from the stables towards the rear entrance of the house. Once she went for a sickening skid, floundered wildly for a moment before he caught hold of her, amazingly surefooted in the quagmire.

At last they reached the back door, pushing it open and making for the mudroom cum first-aid room.

'While you take a shower I'll hunt you up some clothes,' Allegra told him, gasping from exertion 'That's if you don't mind wearing some of the clothes Mark left here? I was going to give them away. But so far I haven't got around to it.'

'Sentimental reasons?' He was busy pulling off his muddy boots.

'No,' she said shortly.

'I couldn't wear them otherwise.' Now he was stripping off his soaked T-shirt with total unselfconsciousness, throwing in the tub before he turned back to her. His eyes blazed like diamonds in his dynamic face. His hair was like black silk. A beautiful man. 'Sure there's nothing of yours I could wear?' he joked, putting up both hands to skim back that wet hair.

Her heart skipped a beat and her blood coursed to her most sensitive places. She wasn't sure how she liked him best. Dressed or undressed? Hell, she couldn't just stand there admiring him, though she actually felt like taking the grand tour around him. Instead she managed a laugh. 'We're not really of a size. Don't worry, everything's clean. You can't imagine how fastidious Mark is. Most of the stuff is brand-new.'

'Beggars can't be choosers,' he said, running a careless hand over his wet chest, a gesture she found incredibly erotic.

'There are clean towels in the cupboard.' Never in her life had she drunk in the sight of a man's body like this. 'Everything you need is there. Don't get under the shower before I come back.'

'Why not?' He shot her a questioning glance..

'Naked men make me uncomfortable,' she joked.

He laughed aloud, looking wonderfully vital. 'Really? And ou an ex-married woman! Surely you saw a naked man on daily basis? Anyway there is such a thing as a towel. I assure ou I'd have one at the ready. The last thing I want to do is row you into a panic. I'll sit right here.' He turned, present-g the wide, gleaming fan of his tanned back and pulled up chair. Then he sat on it, back to front, aiming his wonder- smile at her.

How had this man got so close to her? Why had she let him? *You didn't have a choice.*

Yet he could cast her adrift. Anything was possible in life. it for now, he was making her feel things she had never felt fore. She had to will herself to move. 'Won't be long.' She d already taken off her boots and used a towel to mop up e worst of the mud, now she padded towards the doorway ading into the hall. 'Not much chance of your driving back Jimboorie.' She half turned back. 'Not in this!'

'So what are you saying, I can stay?' His tone was disturb-gly mocking, even erotic.

She held his gaze as long as she could, shocked by the enching physical sensations in her body. She wasn't a hoolgirl with a crush on the captain of the football team. She us an experienced woman, twenty-seven years old. 'Well u're welcome to bolt if you think it's too risky,' she said tartly.

'Never!'

Rory offered up a silent prayer.

And lead me not into temptation.

'I'll stay,' he said. 'Thank you most kindly, Allegra. It'll ve us the opportunity to have a good long chat.'

ry washed out his gear and threw it in the dryer. Then he ned to examining Mark Hamilton's clothing most care-

fully. Everything Allegra had selected was brand-new ar
fine quality. He read the labels. From the dark blue polo shi
to the beige cotton trousers and the classy underpants. He tri
to visualise Allegra's ex-husband. Couldn't. Chloe had calle
him a 'lovely guy' handsome and clever. Was he *all* of tho
things? Allegra in a driven moment had called him a clow
What did that mean exactly? A man forever playing innoc
ous but annoying practical jokes? A man not seriously minde
enough for her? He had to be impaired in some way. He w
a poor lover? He was a violent lover? Clown didn't sou
violent. Who knew what went on inside a marriage anyway
Besides he couldn't trust Chloe. Chloe had made an art for
out of putting down her exquisite sister.

Hamilton was a heavier build. And some inches shorte
The shirt was okay. He had to hitch up the trousers with h
own belt. Rory was much leaner through the waist and hip
The length fell short but okay, who cared? She had even four
him a pair of expensive leather loafers that fitted well enoug
He took a look in the mirror, thrust back his damp hair a
laughed. He had never worn a shirt of such a wondro
electric-blue.

'Gosh you look like someone famous!' Allegra swallow
when she caught sight of him.

'Don't say a rock star.' He grimaced. 'The blue makes n
look swarthier than usual.' He glanced down at the shirt.

'Far from it. It's great. You're a good-looking gu
Compton.' She led the way into the kitchen. 'I could find y
work tomorrow.'

'You surely can't mean as a male model?'

'You want to check out what they're earning,' she retorte
'The guys who get to model here and overseas earn a fortun

'No, thanks. For better or worse I'm buying Naroom. A
we need is the paperwork done.'

'And Valerie's and Chloe's okay,' she tacked on.

'Consider that a fait accompli.' He watched her take salad ingredients out of the crisper in the refrigerator.

'What are we having?'

'Something easy,' she said. 'Steak and salad and maybe some French fries. This afternoon was pretty strenuous.'

'I did warn you.' He let his gaze rest on her, feeling a surge of desire. She had teamed a delicate little lilac top, which looked like silk—he had a mad urge to feel it—with a flowing skirt. Her beautiful hair streamed over her shoulders and down her back, drying in long loose waves. There wouldn't be a man alive who wouldn't get a buzz from simply looking at her, he thought. She was just so effortlessly beautiful. Exclusive looking yet she had worked tirelessly that afternoon. Tirelessly and extremely well. This might be a woman who looked like an orchid but she didn't hesitate to pitch in. He found himself full of admiration for her. She was a woman of surprises.

'Valerie and Chloe were prepared to say yes to $3.5 million,' he reminded her, picking up the conversation. 'Thanks to you they get more.'

She took two prime T-bone steaks from the refrigerator and put them down on the counter before turning to him. Her expression was brushed with worry. 'Valerie said she was going to consult a solicitor with a view to contesting the will.'

'In what way?' He could see that upset her.

'Dad left me a half share of everything,' she said, 'whereas Valerie and Chloe had quarter shares.'

'Tough,' he said, thinking she didn't have a problem. 'I'm no lawyer but I'm willing to bet your father left his will airtight. Don't worry, Allegra. I'd say Valerie was trying to make you suffer. You can bet your life she's already been on to a solicitor who's told her she hasn't a chance in hell of contesting the will. You won't be embroiled in any lawsuit and this deal will go through more smoothly than you think.'

'I don't really want it to go through,' she confessed, leaning against the table.

'Which part of me don't you like?' He stared at her hard.

'This is *home*, Rory.' She met his challenging gaze. 'My father brought my mother here as a bride. I was born here. Even when I was away from it I still *lived* here, if you know what I mean?'

'I surely do.' He thought she put it well.

'To be honest I'd like to die here.'

He stirred restlessly at that. 'Don't for God's sake talk about dying,' he said tersely. 'You've got a long life in front of you. Would you want to stay here and work it?'

'I *could* do it,' she said. 'I'd have to sack guys like Gallagher and Evans and hire some good men. Then I'd see if I could get our old overseer back.'

'Well, well, well,' he said. 'Like I said, you're a *most* surprising woman. But then I don't know a lot about women. I grew up mostly in an all male environment. Even so I'm sure you're very unusual. Do you have the money to buy your step mother and Chloe out?'

She lowered her head, picked up a shiny red capsicum and set it down again 'No, unfortunately. I didn't take penny off Mark.'

'You were entitled to.'

'No.' She shook her head. 'I didn't want to do anything like that. He didn't want to break up the marriage. *I* did.'

'So he was the innocent party?'

'No he wasn't, Rory Compton,' she said with sharp censure. '*I* was the innocent party but don't worry about it. thought maybe I could borrow like you.'

'Really?' He sat back, his hands locked behind his head

'You could try but maybe you wouldn't be so successful,' he warned her. 'You're a woman and you have no real hands on experience.'

'All right, I know that!' she said, giving in to irritation.

'And what about your big city job? I thought you intended going back to it? Surely you'd miss city life? I mean it couldn't be a more different world?'

'Rory, I love the land,' she told him passionately. 'I know it's a little unusual my making such a success of being a fashion editor, but that's only a little part of me. I doubt I would ever have left home had my mother lived. At the beginning living in the city was like living in a foreign country. After life on the land, I felt so hemmed in by all the tall buildings and so many people rushing about. All our space and freedom was lost to me. You should understand.'

'Of course I do.'

She nodded. 'It's not a nice thing to say, but Val drove me away. Val and Chloe to a certain extent. I was made to feel an outsider in my own home.'

'Have you a photograph of your mother?' he asked, sitting straight in his chair again.

She sighed deeply. 'Sure. Wait here.'

Rory rose and walked to the sink feeling vaguely stunned. The last thing he'd expected when they had first met, was such a glamorous young woman would want to live in isolation. In his experience it was men who did that sort of thing. Solitary men who had pioneered the vast interior before admitting women and children to their lives. He knew plenty of reclusives who could only live in the wilderness. Not that the central plains country was anything like wilderness but Naroom was isolated enough. God knows what she'd make of his desert home! Or what had been his desert home he thought with a stab of pain.

His mind wheeling off in several directions, he began to run some of the salad ingredients—tomatoes, cucumber, a bunch of radishes and some celery—under the tap. He could see the mixed salad greens had been prewashed. He felt like that steak. He hoped she had some good English mustard. He was hungry.

Allegra returned a few moments later, holding a large silver framed photograph to her heart.

He held out his hand. Ah, genetics! he thought, much struck by Allegra's striking resemblance to her mother. There were the purely cut features, the shape and set of the eyes, the chin held at a perfect right angle to the neck. There was the same flowing hair, the deep, loose waves. The photograph was black and white but he was certain the hair was the same shade as Allegra's. Even the expression was near identical. Confident, forward-looking, self-assured. Yet this woman had died so tragically young. What a waste!

'It would have been hard for your stepmother to be confronted every day by the image of the woman her husband truly loved?' he spoke musingly, finding it in his heart to pity Valerie.

'Hey, I was only *three* when Val became my stepmother,' Allegra pointed out.

'But the extraordinary resemblance was there. And each year you grew it became more pronounced. By the time you were in your teens you were a powerful rival. Or an ever present reminder if you like.'

She gave him a wounded look. 'Whose side are you on anyway?'

His expression softened. 'I'm sorry, Allegra. I can imagine what it was like for you. In my family Jay took after my father. Physically, that is. Jay is nothing like my father, thank God. I took after my mother. I have her eyes like you have your mother's eyes. Eyes tend to dominate a face. My fathe loved my mother. Or as much as he could love anyone. He sure doesn't love me. I was one terrible reminder she left him. I had to pay for my mother's unforgivable crime.'

'So there's a parallel?' she said more quietly.

'Oddly, yes. Both of us are outsiders.'

The wind and rain kicked up another notch during the night. He awoke to near perfect darkness. Amazingly he had slept. He never thought he would with Allegra sleeping down the hallway. They had talked until after midnight about their lives, their childhood, events that had shaped them, without her ever giving away the reason for abandoning her marriage. He really needed to know. It had become a burning question. Simply put, how could he truly understand until he knew? His mother's abandonment had played such a destructive role in his life he had a natural fear of handing over his heart to a woman who one day might cast him aside. God knows it happened.

Afterwards they had walked around the homestead together like an old married couple, checking all the doors and windows. Only the sexual tension both refused to let get out of bounds, betrayed them. Their hands had only to come into fleeting contact for Rory's hard muscled body to melt like hot wax. He wanted her. He wasn't such a fool he didn't know she wanted him. Sexual magnetism. Each was irresistibly drawn to the other, yet each was determined to keep control. Besides, there were dangers in acting on the most basic, powerful instinct.

Something had caused him to come awake. Some noise in the house. Downstairs. Maybe they should have made the French doors more secure by closing the exterior shutters? The verandah did, however, have a deep protective overhang. He stood up, pulling on his jeans, which he had removed from the dryer earlier in the night. He opened the bedroom door and looked down the corridor. All was quiet. Why wouldn't she be sleeping after such an exhausting afternoon? They had shared a bottle of red wine as well.

It turned out to be what he expected—one of the French doors in the living room. It was rattling loudly as the wind blew against it. He opened one side, latched in back, then stepped out onto the verandah, feeling the invigorating lash of the moisture laden wind. It felt marvellous! Rain to the man on the land was a miracle. The most precious commodity. In the Outback it was either drought or flood. He knew the creek would be in muddy flood by now. Thank God he'd arrived when he had. A woman no matter how willing to chip in wasn't meant to do backbreaking station work.

It took him only moments to secure the shutters, then the interior doors. One of the bolts on the door had worked its way loose, hence the rattle. He padded back into the entrance hall a little disoriented in a strange house. There was less illumination now that he had pulled the shutters. What he had to do was turn on a few lights before he blundered into something and woke Allegra. He didn't think he could cope with seeing her floating towards him on her beautiful high arched feet. He just might grab her, pick her up in his arms, and carry her upstairs…

'God!' He gave a startled oath as a wraithlike figure walked right into instead of through him. He held the apparition by its delicate shoulders.

'Allegra!' He sucked in his breath. Apparitions didn't have warm, satiny flesh.

'Who did you think it was, Chloe back home?' Her voice in the semidarkness came as a soft hiss.

'Out of the question. Chloe's shorter and a lot plumper than you.'

'Don't for God's sake ever call her plump to her face.'

'I wouldn't dream of it. I tried not to wake you.'

'When you were making so much noise?' Her voice rose.

'Pardon me, I was very quiet. Besides, what were trying o do to *me*? For a split second I thought you were a witch.' Very carefully he took his hands off her. Steady. Steady. He ould smell her body scent like some powerful aphrodisiac.

'Witches don't flap around in nighties.'

He was seeing her more and more clearly. 'Are you mad? Of course they do. What's the matter anyway? You're as much ut of breath as if you've been running.'

'I was trying to exercise caution as it happens,' she admon-hed him. 'You gave me a fright, too.'

'Then I'm sorry. There's nothing dangerous about me.'

She laughed shakily. What were they doing here, absorbed a crazy conversation conducted in the near dark? 'I have ews for you, Rory Compton.'

'Better not to tell me. It was one of the French doors. I've osed the shutters. I should have done it before.'

A shiver of excitement came into her voice. 'The wind is uch stronger now.'

It couldn't be stronger than her magnetic pull. Rory mar-elled at his self-control. Maybe honour could explain it? Vhy are you whispering?' he asked.

'I really don't know and I don't want to find out,' she whis-red back. 'We should turn on a light.'

'Damn, why didn't I think of that?'

'The creek will have broken its banks.'

'Any chance of your speaking louder?'

'Oh, shut up!' The tension between then was electrifying. m *so* glad you were here, Rory!'

'*Am* here,' he corrected. 'Now, where the heck *is* the light itch for the stairs?' He knew it was dangerously wrong to keep standing there. Another minute and he'd reach for her. There was only one answer after that.

'I'll get it.' She slipped away like a shadow. Another second and lights bloomed over the stairs and along the upper hallway.

Behind him the tall grandfather clock chimed three.

'Ah, just as I thought!' he exclaimed. 'The witching hour!'

She was standing beneath a glowing wall sconce. It gilded the dark rose of the long hair that framed her face. He saw she was wearing a magical silk robe, a golden-green, with pink and cerise flowers all over it. It had fallen open down the front so he could see her nightgown, the same cerise of the flowers. It gleamed satin. So did the curves of her breasts revealed by the plunging V of the neckline. For a minute his strong legs felt like twigs.

Allegra drew her robe around her, scorchingly aware of his intimate appraisal. She was so aroused she was nearly on fire.

So why aren't you moving?

'We'd better go back to bed,' she said in another furious whisper. 'You go up.'

'Why not leave those two wall sconces on?' he suggested, not wanting and wanting so much to delay her. No words could describe how he felt. There was something magical about her. 'There'll be enough light to see us up the stairs.' He could only wonder at how composed he sounded when his body was flowing with sexual energy.

'The rain seems to be slowing.' She switched off the main lights, then padded on her slippered feet to the base of the stairs. 'Coming?'

He was awed by the electric jolt to his heart. 'Coming where?' He had a sudden overpowering urge to tell her how much he wanted her.

Only she cut him off. 'You *can't* come with *me*!' Her voice trembled. She didn't confess she was terribly tempted.

'I can't help wishing I could.' He stared back at her, hot with hunger. 'Don't be scared, Allegra. I would never offer you a moment's worry.'

She almost burst into tears she was feeling so frustrated. 'I'm not scared of you,' she said. 'I'm scared of me. Haven't we progressed far enough for one night?'

'Years have passed off in a matter of hours,' he said wryly. 'Even then you haven't answered the burning question.'

There was a breathless pause. 'Ask it quickly. I'm going up to bed.' She fixed her jewelled eyes on him.

'What was so wrong with your marriage you had to abandon it?'

She might have turned to marble. 'Don't go there, Rory,' she said.

'You have to get it out of your system.'

She shook her glowing head. 'Believe me, tonight's not the night. Good night, Rory!'

'What's left of it.' He shrugged. 'See you in the morning, Allegra. I'll be up early to check everything's okay.'

'Thank you.' She was already at the first landing, intent on getting to the safety of her bedroom and shutting temptation out. 'If you knock on my door, I'll join you.'

With that she fled.

CHAPTER SIX

THE rain stopped in the predawn .The air was so fresh it was like a liqueur to the lungs. The birds were calling ecstatically to one another secure in the knowledge there was plenty of water. In the orange-red flame of sunrise they drove around the property, Rory at the wheel of the Jeep, revelling in the miracles the rain could perform. Overnight the whole land scape had turned a verdant glowing green. Little purple wild flowers appeared out of nowhere, skittering across the top of the grasses. Hundreds of white capped mushrooms had sprung up beneath the trees that were sprouting tight bunches of edible berries.

They checked on the herd together. It had been little affected by the torrential downpour. The stock had come through the night unscathed and without event. The ha Allegra had feared had not eventuated. Cattle were spread ov all over the sunlit ridges to the rear of the homestead. It wa great to see them so healthy, their liver-red hides washe clean by the downpour.

The creek as expected had burst its banks. They stood a the top of the highest slope looking down at the racing torren It was running strongly, and noisily, carrying a lot of debri fallen branches from the trees and vast clumps of water ree torn up by the flow. When the water hit the big pearl-grey boulders the height reached by the flying spray was something to see. The area around the big rocks churned with swirling eddies of foaming water.

For a time neither of them spoke, simply enjoying the scene and the freshness and fragrance of the early morning. Both of them knew what this life-giving rain meant; how important it was to the entire region. A flight of galahs undulated overhead in a pink and magenta wave. Exquisite little finches were on the wing, brilliantly plumaged lorikeets chasing them out of their territory with weird squawks. Waterfowl, too, were in flight. They came in to the creek to investigate, fanning out over the stream. Allegra and Rory watched as the birds skimmed a few feet above the racing water, then collectively decided it was way too rough to land. They took off as a squadron, soaring steeply back into the sky again. Water was a magnet to birds. They would be back, from all points of the compass just waiting for the raging of the waters to slow and the creek to turn to a splendid landing field.

'Rain, the divine blessing!' Rory breathed as he watched the torrent downstream leap over a rock. 'No rain our way as yet.'

Our way! His beloved Channel Country. They had listened to the radio for news. The late cyclone that had been developing in the Coral Sea was now threatening the far North. Drought continued to reign in the great South-West.

'When it comes, the creeks, the gullies, the waterholes, the long curving billabongs will all fill up,' he continued in a quiet but compelling voice. 'The billabongs cover over with water lilies. None of your home garden stuff. Huge magnificent blooms. Pink, in one place, the sacred blue lotus in another, lovely creams, a deep pinkish red not unlike the colour of your hair. When the rains come the landscape just doesn't get a drenching, the vast flood plains go under.

'We've been totally isolated on Turrawin before today, surrounded on all sides by a marshy sea. When the storms come they come with a vengeance. It's all on a Wagnerian scale—massive thunderheads back lit by plunging spears of lightning. Getting struck and killed isn't uncommon. We had a neighbour killed in a violent electrical storm a few years back.'

Allegra turned to him, registering the homesickness on his handsome face. 'How are you going to be able to settle here, Rory, when your heart is clearly somewhere else?'

He adjusted his hat to further shade his eyes from a brilliant chink of sunlight that fell through the green canopy. 'I told you, Allegra, I can't go back. My home is lost to me.'

'You couldn't find a suitable property in your own region?'

He gave a humourless laugh. 'I could find one, maybe, but I couldn't pay for one. No way! We're talking two entirely different levels here. Our cattle stations—kingdoms are what they're called and it's not so fanciful—dwarf the runs in this area. I have to start more or less around the middle and work my way up.'

Her brows were a question mark. 'But are you going to be happy doing it?'

'Okay, I understand you.' He shrugged. 'The Channel Country is the place of *my* dreaming. It speaks to my soul like Naroom speaks to yours. This is beautiful country, don't get me wrong. Maybe it hasn't got the haunting quality of the desert, or its incredible charisma, but I'll settle here. I have to.'

'I don't think I'd count on it,' Allegra said, shrugging wryly. 'Your love for your desert home won't be shaken off any more than my father's love for my dead mother. Some loves go so deep nothing and no one can approach them.'

'Thinking twice about selling then?' he asked, filling his eyes with her. Her lissom body was clad in a navy and white top and close fitting jeans No makeup again, save for a pin gloss on her mouth. Her thick hair was woven into a rope like plait. He'd never seen a woman look better.

'Valerie and Chloe, when they return, will demand Naroom be sold,' she answered. 'I don't think we could ask for anyone better than you to take it on. You're an astute, ambitious man. I haven't the slightest doubt you'll make a big success of Naroom. And then you'll move on.' She spoke with a lowered head and saddened eyes.

'Hey, that's quite a few years down the line!' He tried to reassure her. 'But isn't that the way of it, Allegra? One expands, not stands still. Which doesn't mean to say Naroom couldn't and wouldn't remain a valuable link in a chain.'

'How good a cattleman is your brother?' she asked abruptly, moving a step nearer the top of the grassy slope to check it was a log that had smashed into one of the creek boulders and not a lost little calf.

'Jay got pushed into it,' he answered. 'He works as hard as any man. Harder, but—'

'He wasn't born to the job,' she cut in gently.

'I told you he wanted to be a doctor. It's a bit late but he could still be. I wouldn't know but he was a straight A student. Jay has a more sensitive side to him than I have.'

She gazed at him out of her black fringed eyes. 'I don't know if that's exactly right. I haven't had the pleasure of meeting Jay, but I would describe you as pretty deep, Rory Compton. You display your sensitivities in many ways.'

'As when?' he asked the question, then broke off abruptly, seized by a mild panic. 'Don't move,' he ordered. 'You could take a tumble.'

Even as he spoke the ground shifted beneath Allegra's feet. 'Oh…hell!' She threw out an arm. He grabbed it strongly, but the soles of her riding boots were slick with grass and mud. She slipped further down the bank with Rory straining to hold her. Allegra almost righted herself, about to thank him for his help, but in the next second a section of rain impacted earth gave way and the two of them began to roll over and over down the wet grassy slope, gathering momentum as they went. Their bodies crushed the multitude of unidentifiable little flowers that grew there in abundance, releasing a sweet musky smell.

Allegra, though powerfully shocked by their tumble, was experiencing a rush of emotions that included exhilaration and a blazing excitement. They were going to go into the stream. She knew that even if she couldn't look. It wouldn't be the first time she'd found herself in deep, fast running water. She was a strong swimmer. He would be, too. She didn't even have to consider it. His powerful arms were around her. What did she care if they had to fight the torrent? They were together. She felt like a woman is supposed to feel when she was with one particular man. A man who walked like he owned the earth.

Rory was taking the brunt of it, trying to protect her body from any hurt along the way. They were to an extent cushioned by the thick grasses that gave up a wonderfully pure, herbal aroma. As they careened towards the rushing creek he crushed her to him. He couldn't risk flinging out an arm. That meant taking one from her, but he was straining to gain purchase with his boots. Finally he hooked into something—a tight web of vines—that slowed their mad descent.

Another four feet and he was able to slam a brake on their rough tumble. They rolled in slow motion to a complete stop finding they were almost at the bottom with the roar of the creek in their ears and the near overwhelming scent of crushed vegetation in their nostrils.

'Bloody hell, woman!' It was an eternity of seconds before Rory could speak. Then his words came out explosively. He was poised over her, staring down into her beautiful face vivi

vith exhilaration. 'Just hold it right there!' He held her
aptive, as if he believed her capable of jumping up and taking
 header into the creek just for the hell of it!

She laughed with absolute delight. The sound was crystal
lear. Transparent like an excited child's.

'Why did you stop us?' she wailed. 'I wanted to take a swim.'

'More likely bash your head against a rock,' he told her
ternly.' The current is too strong.'

'Still I enjoyed it, didn't you?' She stared into his glittering
yes. 'I'll remember it for always.' The great thing was, she
neant it. She raised her hand and very slowly caressed his
ronze cheek, taking exquisite pleasure in the fine rasp of his
eard on her skin. She fancied she saw little rays of light around
is head. An energy that held her within his magnetic field?

'So what are you trying to do to me?' Rory stared down at
er, equally bedazzled. 'What a repertoire of alluring little
pells you have!'

'All called up with you in mind.'

'Then there's only one thing left to do.' The last tight coils
f his self-control broke free. He was so hungry for her he
idn't know how he was going to assuage it. He lowered his
ead, intent on capturing her mouth, only to see with a flame
f wonder her lovely mouth ready itself to receive his.

What would he do to her if she let him?

He kissed her very slowly and gently at first until he had her
vhimpering and moving her head from side to side in agitation.
'hen his kisses strengthened in pressure and intensity as his
assion for her surged. What a fool he was thinking he had
chooled himself to restraint. The reality was he was so power-
ally attracted to her he had lost the capacity for rational thought.

Time stopped. The whole world stopped. Pain and old grief
vere forgotten. His weight pinioned her body into the thick,
erdant grasses.

'Am I hurting you?'

'Don't go way.' She loved the weight of him. Her eyelid fluttered shut and she caught the back of his neck with her hand.

He kissed her until both of them were gasping and out of breath. His hands were sliding slowly, sensuously, over her body as though learning it. Sometimes she led his touch, the delicate contours of her breasts swelling at his caress. Her heart felt like it was going to break out from behind her rib cage. Never before in her life had she felt such sensual excitement. Being with him had increased her every perception one hundredfold.

The breeze shook leaves from the trees. They flew down to them, golden-green, purple backed, landing gently in the glowing garnet coils of her hair. If ever a man could take a woman with his eyes he was guilty of taking her now Rory thought. In a minute she would lay her hand on his cheek again and tell him to stop.

Only she didn't.

For a woman who had lived three years in a bad marriage, Allegra felt unbelievably ecstatic. She wasn't unafraid of anything that was in him, because it was in *her*.

'Allegra, do you trust me?' His lips pressed against her throat.

'Do *you* trust *me*?'

Did he trust her siren song? The monumental shift in his line of defence couldn't have been more apparent. 'Do I trust life itself,' he murmured, continuing to trail passionate kisses across her face and throat. 'You must know I want you badly.' How could she not when she had been moving her hand over him as he moved his over her?

Allegra's breathing came fast and shallow. She *had* to tell him before his body took total control of his mind. 'It's not a safe time for me right now, Rory.' She tried to laugh, but couldn't bring it off.

'Oh my God!' He stopped kissing her, his sigh deep and tortured. 'Oh God, Allegra!' Frustration whirled through him with the force of a tornado. 'I'd better let go of you,' he groaned.

'Maybe you'd better.' Her own burning desire was at war with all ideas of caution and common sense. She was panicked by the thought that desire for him could very well win if they didn't move. 'I didn't know all this was going to happen so soon.'

'Hell, don't apologise,' he said, his body racked by painful little stabs. 'So you could fall pregnant?' He helped her to sit up.

'It's a strong possibility.' She held a hand over her heart, trying to quiet her breathing.

'I wish to God I'd brought some protection.' His handsome face was taut with frustration.

'So do I.' She laughed without humour, her creamy skin covered in a fine dew of heat.

'I'm so desperate to get close to you,' he admitted, teetering on the edge of saying a whole lot more.

'Are you?' She turned to stare into his eyes, conscious of a sudden joy.

'You know I am. Damn, damn, damn,' he groaned. 'So what do we do? Let the flames die?'

'It might be a good idea.' She didn't bother to hide her regret.

'Would you *want* to have my baby?' he asked very quietly.

'Are you speaking seriously?' It wouldn't be the end of the world if she fell pregnant to him. It would be thrilling.

'Yes,' he said.

'What's going on in your mind, Rory?' She was trying to read it from his expression.

'You haven't answered the question.'

'I want children,' she said. 'I've told you that before.'

He took her hand, looking intently into her eyes. 'Do you think we have enough going for us to consider marriage?' He knew he was being carried to extremes, but maybe extremism was his natural bent? Either that or he had finally found his life's focus.

'Rory!' Allegra began to laugh a little wildly. For a minute she felt like she was flying; caught up by a great wind. She who had come through a catastrophic relationship was being asked to consider marriage again. What was even more astounding was she knew right away what her decision would be. Something extraordinary had happened to her. She had to seize the day.

'Well?' He took her chin, sparkles of light in his eyes.

'You don't have to propose to me to get me into bed,' she said, pierced by the look in his eyes. She was long used to men regarding her but this was something entirely different.

'You think I don't know that?' he said gently. 'I know this has come at an odd time, but can't you see the beauty of it? I want a family. So do you. We're much the same age. Neither of us is content to let things go on much longer. If I've shocked you with my audacity, perhaps you can think of it as a contract that could work extremely well for both of us as we both have the same aims. You wouldn't have to leave the home you love. You'd gain a half share as my wife and partner. You'd be able to hold onto your own money. It's important for a woman to feel financially independent.'

The words were business-like, but the warmth of real emotion was in the sound. 'I should say you're crazy!' Allegra was still flying high. To share a dream! Isn't that what she had always wanted?

'You know I'm not.'

'So what are you leading us into?' she asked as calmly as she could.

'Why a marriage of convenience for two people who just so happen to suit one another right down to the ground.'

'We can't have love, too?'

For answer, he turned her face to him and dropped a brief, ravishing kiss on her mouth. 'Wouldn't you say we're more than halfway there?'

So there was one secret between them. She was already there. 'Maybe we should slow down instead of full steam ahead?' she suggested before binding him to her.

'I'm going to leave that up to you, Allegra,' he said. '*I* won't change my mind. You're the woman I want.'

She kept her eyes lowered. 'You can't have forgotten both of us have a lot of old issues to work through?'

'We can work through them together.' His response was swift and sure. 'Have I dared too much too soon?' He searched her eyes for any hint of misgiving. 'I hadn't planned any of it. It took a tumble down the hill to shake it out of me. Love is a big word. Maybe the biggest in the dictionary. I don't think we're going to have a problem getting into bed together, do you?' he asked dryly.

No problem at all but she had to remind him. 'There's a bit more to marriage than sex, Rory.'

He nearly said what was flooding his mind. *I love you.* But the last thing he wanted was to frighten her off. 'Do you think I don't know that? We really *like* each other, though, don't we? Not that I'm about to knock great sex. Marriage would be very bad without it. But we have a lot in common. All the things we talked about last night. Our love of the land. Don't let any bad experience you may have had with your husband warp you.'

She felt a frisson of shock. She had never said a word to him about Mark. What then had he assumed? 'So much depends on our mutual love of the land, doesn't it?' she said, ignoring the reference to Mark.

'I'd be lying if I didn't say it was a crucial factor.' He didn't drop his gaze. 'I couldn't consider marrying a woman—no matter how much I wanted her—if I knew she might go off and leave me when the going got rough. Worse, leave our kids. You were being entirely truthful when you said the land is where you belong?'

'Of course! How could you doubt me?' She shook her head vigorously. 'I have my own dreaming.'

'Well then, it's a brilliant idea,' he said as though that clinched it.

'More like explosive!' Allegra knew she ought to be filled with doubts but incredibly she wasn't. She felt more like a woman who had been blind all her life then finally opened her eyes. In fact, she had never felt so good. 'You've got to give me a little time to think,' she said, paying a moment's homage to caution. Impossible to *think* when he was holding her hand and making love to her with his eyes. 'This is scary. Or it darn well ought to be. I didn't do too brilliantly the last time.'

'And you won't let me hear the problem. He didn't abuse you, did he?' Rory couldn't abide the thought. 'I'd go find him and horse whip him if he did.'

'And wind up inside a jail? I wouldn't like that. Mark isn' a violent man. In many respects he's the perfect gentleman Everyone thought so anyway. People can act perfectly civilised but one barely has to scratch the surface to discove they're something quite different underneath. My dad didn' take to Mark. I knew that although Dad never put his concern into words.'

'I'm listening,' he prompted, feeling an iron determination to protect her.

She bent her head, unsure how much to say. 'Mark was int a fantasy life. A *sexual* fantasy life.'

'One that bothered you?' he frowned.

'Once I found out he'd been unfaithful the marriage wa as good as over. I hate to talk about it, actually. I forgave hir the first time. I thought it was a one-off aberration and I fe badly about calling it quits so early in the marriage. But it wasn't. Mark continued his brief encounters with married women in our own circle. They made an absolute fool out of me. Opportunity is always present if one is looking for it.'

'Good God!' Rory made a deep, growling sound in his throat. 'He sounds like an oversexed adolescent.'

Allegra's shrug was cynical. 'A lot of men of all ages fit that description. Men and woman have affairs. Married or not. I saw a lot of it. One can't help attraction. The possibility is always there. If one is married the right decision is to consciously turn away from temptation. Some don't.'

'You never thought to get even?' he asked. 'Sorry, I withdraw that. I know you didn't.'

'You're dead right. I respected my marriage vows. I respected myself. That's why I had to get out.' She steadied herself to look into his eyes. 'I liked the way you checked the minute I said it wasn't the right time to have sex.'

'Why of course! You surely didn't think I would force the issue?'

'I didn't, but I *was* responding an awful lot. In a way it was a crisis and you dealt with it the way it had to be. Mark messed me up for a while. He's quite a bit older. Nearly ten years. He set out to mould me to *his* ways but he failed. He actually believed his little affairs were harmless. He swore over and over he loved only me. I was his *wife*. That put me on a pedestal instead of exposing me to ridicule. He swore he'd get help.'

'And did he?' Rory was having difficulty understanding a man like Mark Hamilton.

'I didn't wait around to find out,' Allegra replied flatly. 'I believed I did at the time, but I didn't love Mark. He was more a replacement father figure. Had I really loved him I'd have been devastated at the divorce, instead of just plain *mad* at myself. The state of my home life—the way I grew up—

pushed me into trying to find someone safe. Mark had every outward appearance of being safe, except he wasn't safe at all. I made one hell of a mistake. I can't possibly make another.' She was too close to tears to say another word.

He drew her within the haven of his arm.' Did you tell your stepmother and Chloe about this?'

She nodded. 'But not all that much. They thought the world of Mark. In their eyes if anyone was to blame for the break-down of our marriage it was me. Val has been compelled to find fault with me since I was a kid. I couldn't do a thing right. She used to make up stories for Chloe to believe and Chloe did. I used to be devastated. Not anymore. Over the years, Val has brainwashed my sister. Chloe would be a much better person away from her mother. In her heart Chloe knows it. Anyway there's nothing I can do there. It's all too late. There's a lot of deep resentment. Not love.'

'Was there *any* happiness in your marriage?' he asked.

'I can remember some good times,' she said. 'At the be-ginning.'

'Then let me make up for all you've missed.' His hand slid to her nape, cradling her head. He allowed himself the sheer bliss of kissing her again, only breaking it by force of will. 'You'll have to be really, *really* patient for the rest.' Mockery sparkled in his eyes.

'I guess I have to be okay with that.' Her voice was soft. He had taken her breath. Sunlight was filtering through the trees, warming them in its streams of golden light.

'I suppose we could live together first like couples do these days?' He put forward the idea as a way of giving her an option. 'Does that appeal to you? A trial run? We could take it in stages if that would make you feel easier in your mind You can have all the time you want to get used to me. The same goes for me.' He gave a sardonic ripple of laughter

'Although I'll never get used to you if I live a hundred years.' She had stopped him in his tracks when he had first laid eyes on her. She was even more beautiful to him now.

'You'll make some woman a terrific husband, Rory Compton,' she told him, thus stating her clear preference.

'Then that woman better be *you*!'

CHAPTER SEVEN

VALERIE'S face was a study. She jumped to her feet, moving towards Allegra as though she would like to slap her. 'How long now is it since your divorce and you're planning to *remarry*?' Her voice rang so loudly it bounced off the walls. 'Even knowing you the way I do, I can scarcely believe it.'

Chloe sat trembling, on the verge of tears. 'What did you *do* when we were away?' she demanded to know, her voice sounding thick in a clogged throat.

'Do?' Allegra repeated. She fell back from the kitchen table, as ever feeling outnumbered. 'I hardly think it's got a damned thing to do with you, Chloe. You should be thrilled I managed to get extra for Naroom, instead of questioning me like this. I haven't heard a word about the better offer.'

'Did you sleep with him?' Valerie threw out an arm so precipitously she knocked over a glass on the sink. It smashed on the terracotta tiles but all three women ignored it.

Allegra sat there wondering why after all these years, she was still stunned by their reactions. 'That's absolutely none of your business.'

A dark look crossed Valerie's face and her jaw set hard. 'I bet you did. You take no notice of the conventions. Mark was too much the gentleman to say a word against you.'